BOOK 7 OF THE
ADULT LEARNER SERIES

Nightmare Snow

JUDITH ANDREWS GREEN
DIRECTOR,
OXFORD HILLS ADULT AND
COMMUNITY EDUCATION
SCHOOL ADMINISTRATIVE DISTRICT #17
SOUTH PARIS, MAINE

JAMESTOWN PUBLISHERS
PROVIDENCE, RHODE ISLAND

Catalog No. 206

Nightmare Snow

 Address all inquiries to Editor, Jamestown Publishers, Post Office Box 9168, Providence, Rhode Island 02940.

Cover and Story Illustrations by
Bob Giuliani

Printed in the United States AL

88 89 90 9 8 7 6 5 4 3 2

ISBN 0-89061-283-8

Titles in This Series

No. 200, Murder by Radio
No. 201, The Man Who Stopped Time
No. 202, The Man with the Scar
No. 203, Dr. Valdez
No. 204, The Secret of Room 401
No. 205, A City for Ransom
No. 206, Nightmare Snow
No. 207, Peril on the Road
No. 208, Killer in a Trance?

In memory of
Terry Hauck—Brown-Pembroke Outing Club
and
Chris Rounds—Franklin County International Club
and to all the members of those clubs

To the Reader

Ted thought that climbing a mountain in the winter would be easy. The weather was good. His friends were good hikers. What could happen?

He didn't know that his nightmares were trying to tell him something.

What was it? Read on in *Nightmare Snow* to find out.

Before each chapter of the story, there are words for you to read and learn. The words are given in sentences, so that you can see how they will be used in the story. After each chapter there are questions for you to answer. Those questions will give you an idea of how well you are reading.

Also following each chapter is a section called Language Skills. It has lessons that will help you to read, write and spell better.

The last two parts of each unit deal with Life Skills. Life skills are things you need to know about and know how to do to get along in life.

The answers to all the questions and exercises are in the back of the book. You can check your answers to see if they are right.

We hope you will like reading *Nightmare Snow* and learning all the things this book teaches.

Contents

How to Use This Book

***Preview Words**/Chapter 1*

Study the words in the box. Then read the sentences below with your teacher. Look carefully at the words in boldface type.

apartment	frostbite	meadow	snowshoes
breakfast	heavy	Mickey Mouse	sparkles
climbed	hiker	nightmare	station
dreaming	jacket	puffed	weather
excited	lovely	sign	wrong

1. Ted was **dreaming** that he was lost in the snow.
2. What a **nightmare**! It had seemed so real!
3. Ted got dressed and had a quick **breakfast**.
4. We'll get you a good, warm **jacket**.
5. Wait till you see how the sun **sparkles** on the snow.
6. They went to Cathy's **apartment**.
7. Ted thought they had gone to the **wrong** apartment.
8. He's a good **hiker**.
9. You don't want to lose a mitten. You would get **frostbite**.
10. We call them **Mickey Mouse** boots.
11. But I've never used **snowshoes**!
12. This backpack is **heavy**!
13. It was a **lovely** place.
14. We'll go up across this big, open **meadow**.
15. If the **weather** is good, we'll get up to the top of the mountain.
16. The jacket **puffed** up as he pulled on it.
17. Ted began to feel **excited**.
18. The others were waiting in Cathy's **station** wagon.
19. He **climbed** into the back seat.
20. I hope it isn't a bad **sign**.

1. Learn the Preview Words

Say the words in the box. Then read the sentences. Try to learn the words. See if you know what each sentence means.

***Too Big to Move**/Chapter 1*

Ted was dreaming. He was dreaming that he was lost in the snow. All around him was snow. He couldn't see anything but snow. Everywhere he looked—snow, snow, snow.

And the wind! The wind beat against him. The wind blew the snow into his face, into his eyes. It pushed him back. He put his head down against the wind and tried to move on. He had to go on!

But it was so cold. So cold. And he was so tired of fighting against the deep snow and the wind. He was so tired that he wanted just to lie down and rest. Lie down in the deep, soft snow and go to sleep. The snow would cover him up, and he would be warm. He would lie down, and the snow would cover him.

And he would die.

Ted woke up with a start. He sat up in bed, shaking with cold and fear. What a nightmare that had been! It had seemed so real! He couldn't shake off the feeling of being lost in the snow.

He rubbed his hands across his eyes and then looked over at his clock. It was almost 10:30 already. No wonder he had been dreaming—he wasn't used to sleeping so late in the morning.

He got up and walked around the room, trying to get the nightmare out of his head. He walked over to the window and looked out. It sure didn't look like his nightmare out there! There wasn't much snow on the ground, and the city streets looked cold and bare and dirty.

Ted turned away from the window. Winter! He hated

2. Read the Chapter

As you read, try to follow the events of the story. See if you can guess what the nightmare means.

***Comprehension Questions**/Chapter 1*

Directions. Answer these questions about the chapter you have just read. Put an *x* in the box beside the best answer to each question.

1. (D) How did Ted feel when he woke up from his nightmare?
   - ☐ a. He was happy that it was over.
   - ☐ b. He wanted to go back to sleep.
   - ☐ c. He was scared and upset.
   - ☐ d. He felt like a fool.

2. (C) What did Dennis do first?
   - ☐ a. He took Ted to the camping store.
   - ☐ b. He talked Ted into going on the camping trip.
   - ☐ c. He had supper at the girls' apartment.
   - ☐ d. He helped Ted pack his backpack.

3. (A) Dennis said, "In winter, you have the woods *all to yourself*." What does this mean?
   - ☐ a. Ted owns the woods.
   - ☐ b. There are no other people in the woods.
   - ☐ c. Ted will see every tree.
   - ☐ d. Ted must go on the camping trip alone.

3. Answer: Comprehension Questions

Put an *x* in the box next to the best answer to each question. Read all ten questions first and answer the easy ones. Then go back and answer the hard ones.

4. *Correct Your Answers*

Use the Answer Key on page 209. Circle any answers you got wrong, and mark the right answers with an *x*.

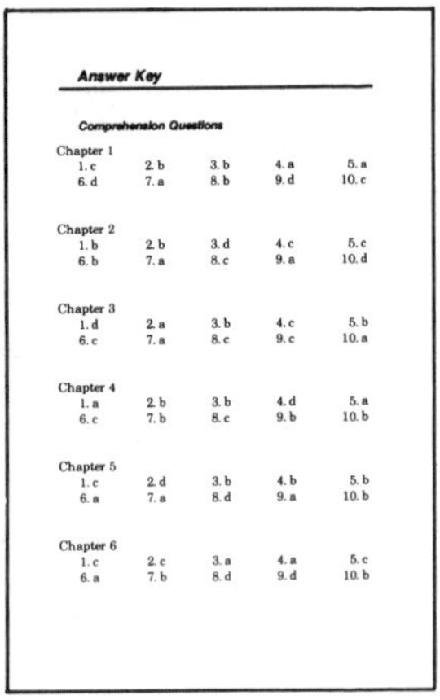

Answer Key

Comprehension Questions

Chapter 1	1. c	2. b	3. b	4. a	5. a
	6. d	7. a	8. b	9. d	10. c
Chapter 2	1. b	2. b	3. d	4. c	5. c
	6. b	7. a	8. c	9. a	10. d
Chapter 3	1. d	2. a	3. b	4. c	5. b
	6. c	7. a	8. c	9. c	10. a
Chapter 4	1. a	2. b	3. b	4. d	5. a
	6. c	7. b	8. c	9. b	10. b
Chapter 5	1. c	2. d	3. b	4. b	5. b
	6. a	7. a	8. d	9. a	10. b
Chapter 6	1. c	2. c	3. a	4. a	5. c
	6. a	7. b	8. d	9. d	10. b

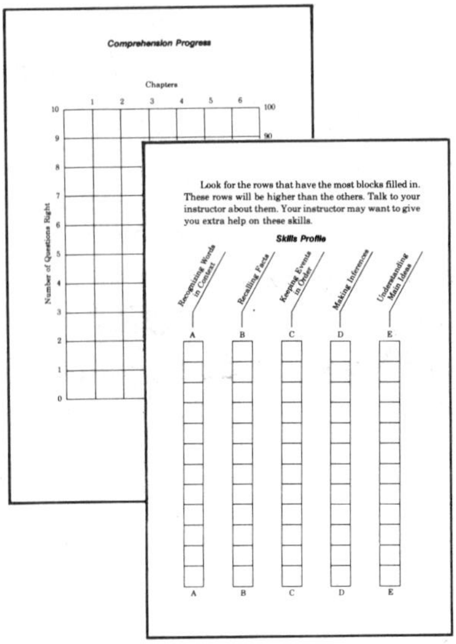

5. *Fill in the Graphs*

Fill in the graph on page 221 to show your comprehension score. Use the graph on page 223 to chart your skills.

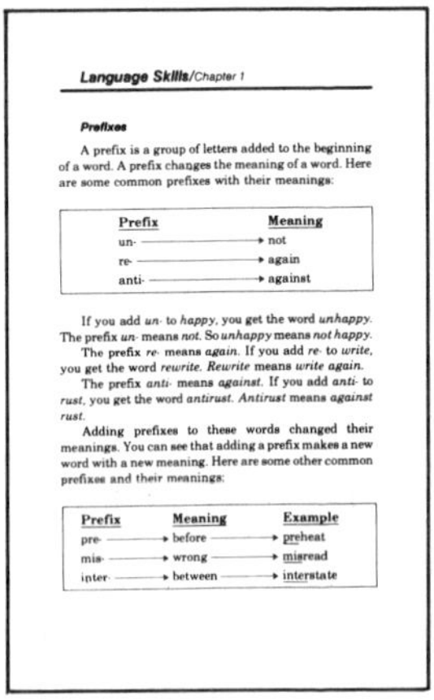

Language Skills/Chapter 1

Prefixes

A prefix is a group of letters added to the beginning of a word. A prefix changes the meaning of a word. Here are some common prefixes with their meanings:

Prefix	Meaning
un- →	not
re- →	again
anti- →	against

If you add *un-* to *happy*, you get the word *unhappy*. The prefix *un-* means *not*. So *unhappy* means *not happy*.

The prefix *re-* means *again*. If you add *re-* to *write*, you get the word *rewrite*. *Rewrite* means *write again*.

The prefix *anti-* means *against*. If you add *anti-* to *rust*, you get the word *antirust*. *Antirust* means *against rust*.

Adding prefixes to these words changed their meanings. You can see that adding a prefix makes a new word with a new meaning. Here are some other common prefixes and their meanings:

Prefix	Meaning	Example
pre- →	before →	preheat
mis- →	wrong →	misread
inter- →	between →	interstate

6. *Read: Language Skills*

This comes after the questions. Read the pages and do the exercises. Use the Answer Key that begins on page 210 to correct the exercises.

7. Read: Understanding Life Skills

Read these pages and follow the step-by-step lessons. Use the Answer Key that begins on page 214 to check your answers.

Understanding Life Skills/*Chapter 1*

Local Phone Numbers

You probably use the telephone every day. Most of the time, you telephone people in your town or city. The area around your own town or city is called the *local area*. When you call someone in this area, you are making a *local call*.

To make a local call, you must use a phone number. A local phone number looks like this: 421-8162. You can find local phone numbers in the *telephone book*. The telephone book will have numbers for people and for businesses.

Here is part of a page from a phone book:

Ancone Linda 146 Russell St Brgfld **723-6418**
Anderson Arthur E 31 General St Bngr **332-9216**
Anderson Arthur P 183 Manson Ave Dumnt ... **384-3384**
Anderson J 82 Sunny Cove Dr Scit **749-1351**
Anderson M 22 Garfield Av Tnck **721-1983**
Andrade Esther 334 Dionne St Montvl **529-4427**
Barber CA 5 Red St Lewstn **461-1179**
Bennett John N 57 Pembroke Dr Brkln **739-2527**
Cardoso Jose 268 Florence Rd Upton **863-6942**

Each line in the phone book tells you three things. It tells you a person's *name*. It tells you a person's *address*. It tells you a person's *phone number*. Here is what one line looks like:

last name	first name	middle initial	street address	town or city	phone number
Bennett	**John**	**N**	57 Pembroke Dr	Brkln	739-2527

Shortened Words

You can see that some of the words in this line from the phone book have letters left out. The letters are left

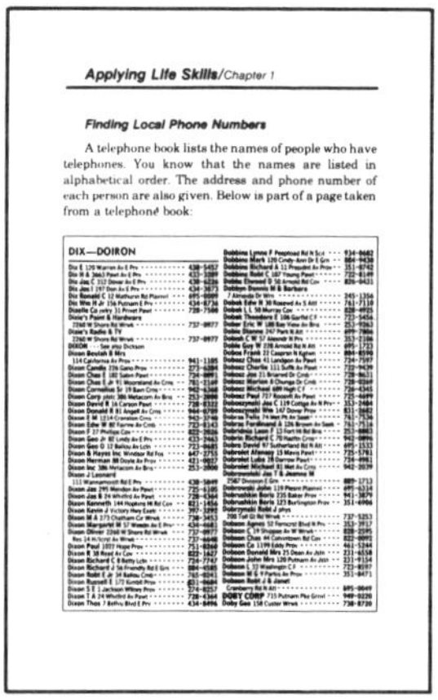

Applying Life Skills/*Chapter 1*

Finding Local Phone Numbers

A telephone book lists the names of people who have telephones. You know that the names are listed in alphabetical order. The address and phone number of each person are also given. Below is part of a page taken from a telephone book:

DIX—DOIRON

8. Practice: Applying Life Skills

Read the instructions and do the Life Skills exercise. Take your time. Do the work carefully. Try to remember what you just read about understanding life skills. Use the Answer Key that begins on page 216 to correct the exercise.

9. Read the Chapter Again

Go back to the story and read it once more. This time as you read, try to feel all the interest and excitement the writer has built in.

Then go on to the Preview Words for the next chapter.

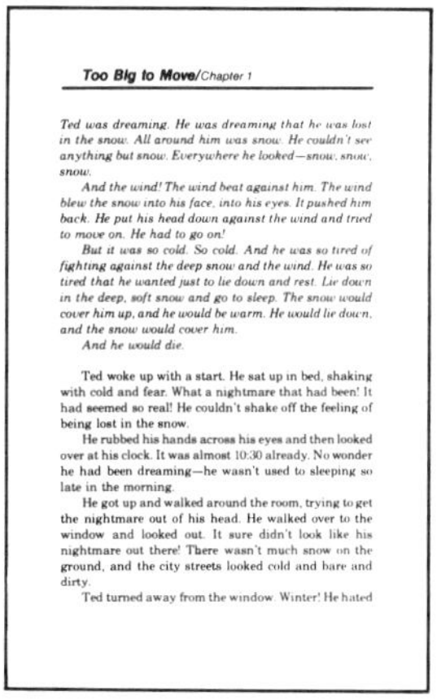

Too Big to Move/*Chapter 1*

Ted was dreaming. He was dreaming that he was lost in the snow. All around him was snow. He couldn't see anything but snow. Everywhere he looked—snow, snow, snow.

And the wind! The wind beat against him. The wind blew the snow into his face, into his eyes. It pushed him back. He put his head down against the wind and tried to move on. He had to go on!

But it was so cold. So cold. And he was so tired of fighting against the deep snow and the wind. He was so tired that he wanted just to lie down and rest. Lie down in the deep, soft snow and go to sleep. The snow would cover him up, and he would be warm. He would lie down, and the snow would cover him.

And he would die.

Ted woke up with a start. He sat up in bed, shaking with cold and fear. What a nightmare that had been! It had seemed so real! He couldn't shake off the feeling of being lost in the snow.

He rubbed his hands across his eyes and then looked over at his clock. It was almost 10:30 already. No wonder he had been dreaming—he wasn't used to sleeping so late in the morning.

He got up and walked around the room, trying to get the nightmare out of his head. He walked over to the window and looked out. It sure didn't look like his nightmare out there! There wasn't much snow on the ground, and the city streets looked cold and bare and dirty.

Ted turned away from the window. Winter! He hated

1

Too Big to Move

Preview Words/*Chapter 1*

Study the words in the box. Then read the sentences below with your teacher. Look carefully at the words in boldface type.

apartment	frostbite	meadow	snowshoes
breakfast	heavy	Mickey Mouse	sparkles
climbed	hiker	nightmare	station
dreaming	jacket	puffed	weather
excited	lovely	sign	wrong

1. Ted was **dreaming** that he was lost in the snow.
2. What a **nightmare**! It had seemed so real!
3. Ted got dressed and had a quick **breakfast**.
4. We'll get you a good, warm **jacket**.
5. Wait till you see how the sun **sparkles** on the snow.
6. They went to Cathy's **apartment**.
7. Ted thought they had gone to the **wrong** apartment.
8. He's a good **hiker**.
9. You don't want to lose a mitten. You would get **frostbite**.
10. We call them **Mickey Mouse** boots.
11. But I've never used **snowshoes**!
12. This backpack is **heavy**!
13. It was a **lovely** place.
14. We'll go up across this big, open **meadow**.
15. If the **weather** is good, we'll get up to the top of the mountain.
16. The jacket **puffed** up as he pulled on it.
17. Ted began to feel **excited**.
18. The others were waiting in Cathy's **station** wagon.
19. He **climbed** into the back seat.
20. I hope it isn't a bad **sign**.

Ted was dreaming.

He was dreaming that he was lost in the snow. All around him was snow. He couldn't see anything but snow. Everywhere he looked—snow, snow, snow.

And the wind! The wind beat against him. The wind blew the snow into his face, into his eyes. It pushed him back. He put his head down against the wind and tried to move on. He had to go on!

But it was so cold. So cold. And he was so tired of fighting against the deep snow and the wind. He was so tired that he wanted just to lie down and rest. Lie down in the deep, soft snow and go to sleep. The snow would cover him up, and he would be warm. He would lie down, and the snow would cover him.

And he would die.

Ted woke up with a start. He sat up in bed, shaking with cold and fear. What a nightmare that had been! It had seemed so real! He couldn't shake off the feeling of being lost in the snow.

He rubbed his hands across his eyes and then looked over at his clock. It was almost 10:30 already. No wonder he had been dreaming—he wasn't used to sleeping so late in the morning.

He got up and walked around the room, trying to get the nightmare out of his head. He walked over to the window and looked out. It sure didn't look like his nightmare out there! There wasn't much snow on the ground, and the city streets looked cold and bare and dirty.

Ted turned away from the window. Winter! He hated

winter! Winter was cold and snow and nothing to do. Even sleeping wasn't much fun if he had nightmares!

Summer—now, that was another story. On warm summer nights, he would take long walks all over the city. And in summer, if he felt like it, he could get right out of the city and go camping. He could pack up his sleeping bag and some food and take off with his friends, out to the woods where it was quiet. Yes, summer was the best time for Ted.

But now it was winter, and he hated every minute of it!

He got dressed and had a quick breakfast. Then he looked around his apartment for something to do. He sat down and tried to read a book, but he couldn't sit still. He couldn't get that nightmare out of his head.

"Does it mean something?" Ted asked himself. "I've never had a nightmare that seemed so real. I feel as if it's trying to tell me something. No, that's crazy! How could a dream tell me anything? I just need to get out for a while."

He put on his coat and went down the stairs. As he stepped out the front door, the wind hit him, pulling at his hat and blowing down inside his coat. He pulled his coat up tightly under his chin and walked down the street with a big frown on his face, kicking at the dirty snow that lay along the sidewalk. What a nothing day!

He stopped at the corner and waited for the light to change. As the wind blew down the street, Ted felt as if it were blowing right through him. "Hurry up, light!" he said. "Hurry up and change!"

"Talking to yourself?" someone behind him asked.

Ted turned around to see who had talked to him. "Oh it's you, Dennis. I haven't seen you in a long time. How's it going?"

"Great!" Dennis said. "But what's wrong with you?

You should see your face! If you walk around with a frown like that, you'll scare little kids on the street! What's wrong?"

"Oh nothing, really. Too much winter, that's all. I've been laid off from work for a week, and I have nothing to do. But what are *you* so happy about?"

"I'm going camping!" Dennis grinned.

"Camping? In the winter? Are you crazy?"

"No, it's great! I'm going with Cathy and Emily. You know them, don't you? A guy named John White is coming too. We're leaving tomorrow, and we're planning to be gone for five days."

Ted shook his head. "Maybe I didn't hear you right. Or maybe you just haven't looked around you lately," he said, pointing down the cold city street. He felt cold inside as he remembered that nightmare again.

"Camping in the winter is great!" Dennis was saying. "It's really quiet. You have the woods all to yourself. And the woods are so pretty in the snow. Say—would you like to come along? Another girl was going to come, but now she can't make it, so we have room in the car. And we could use your tent! Come on, I'm just on my way to meet the others. They'd be glad to have you come along!"

"But . . . I hate the cold!" Ted started to say. But just then the light changed. Dennis stepped off the sidewalk and started to cross the street, so that Ted had to hurry to catch up with him.

"You'll love it!" Dennis was saying. "All that nice, clean, white snow and the nice, quiet woods. The air is so fresh and clean. You'll love it!"

"But I'll be cold!" Ted said. Maybe this was what the dream was trying to tell him! No, he told himself, that was crazy.

"You won't be cold," Dennis said. "We'll get you a

good jacket. I think John has an extra one you could use. You can rent some boots from a camping store. Just wait till you see how the sun sparkles on the deep snow. It's really something!"

"But . . . but . . . I can't just run off like this," Ted said as he hurried along beside Dennis. But he already knew he was going on that camping trip. He wasn't going to let a nightmare scare him.

They went to the apartment that Cathy and Emily shared with another girl. Ted had been there once for a party. But when Cathy opened the door, Ted thought that they had gone to the wrong apartment. The place was a mess! Things were piled up everywhere. Boxes and bags and boots and jackets and mittens—everywhere he looked, Ted saw more things.

"Hi, Dennis, come on in," Cathy said. "Hi, Ted, I haven't seen you since our party last fall. How are you? Come on in and have a seat—if you can find one." She pushed a jacket off a chair onto the floor. Ted sat down on the chair and looked around him.

"Is all this stuff for your camping trip?" he asked. "Are you going for five days, or five years?"

"Oh, we'll use it all," Cathy smiled. "You have to be ready for anything in the winter. And you eat a lot more when you're out in the cold."

"Eating!" Emily called from the other room. "That's what I like about winter camping. You can eat and eat, and you never get fat!"

"Is *that* why you do it!" Cathy said. "Then *you* come out here and work on the food."

"Ted is going to come with us," Dennis said. "OK?"

"Well, I'm not sure . . ." Cathy started to say.

"Oh he's all right," Dennis cut in. "I've been hiking with him lots of times. He's a good hiker, and he knows what he's doing in the woods."

"That's fine, then," Cathy said. "The more people we have, the more fun we'll have. And when I got the food I got extra, because I thought that Sue was coming. So everything will work out just fine."

"And Ted has a tent!" Dennis said.

"Oh good," Cathy said, "that takes care of that problem."

"But I'm not sure that . . ." Ted began.

"He's never been winter camping before," Dennis went on, "so he'll need a jacket and some boots. And I'll bet he'll need a sleeping bag. Ted, do you have a winter sleeping bag?"

"No, my sleeping bag isn't very warm."

"You'll need a winter bag. I have a friend who can lend you one. Look, I'll take you to a camping store to rent some boots. Then we'll go back to your apartment, and I'll help you pack so that we can be sure you have everything you need. Come on," Dennis said as he walked out the door. "See you later, Cathy."

Ted hurried after Dennis. What a day! First there was nothing to do, and now he was running around with too much to do.

He forgot all about the nightmare.

When they got to the camping store, Dennis picked out a pair of mittens for Ted. "They're so big!" Ted said. "And look, they have a string on them! I haven't had a string on my mittens since I was a little kid."

"You don't want to lose a mitten out there," Dennis said. You would lose the hand, too. You would get frostbite."

Then Ted saw his boots—big black rubber things. "I can't walk in those!" he shouted.

"They aren't as bad as they look," Dennis said, "and

no one has ever had frostbite in these. We call them Mickey Mouse boots."

"Because they look just like Mickey Mouse's big feet, right? And I'm going to *feel* like Mickey Mouse when I wear them."

"But you'll be warm," Dennis said. "Now what about snowshoes? No one has any spare snowshoes, so you'll have to rent those, too."

"But I've never used snowshoes," Ted said.

"There's nothing to it. You just walk," Dennis said.

"Couldn't I get along without them?"

"In snow up to your neck? No, you can't get along without them. Now let's see . . . boots, mittens, snowshoes . . . that should do it. Let's go."

When they got to Ted's apartment, Dennis helped Ted pick out what he would need for five days. Then he helped him pack it all into his backpack.

Ted lifted the backpack and groaned. "This thing is *heavy!*" he said. "It must be fifty or sixty pounds already! When I get my share of the food in there, I'm not sure I'm going to be able to pick it up. And then you think I'm going to *carry* it somewhere? On snowshoes? You've got to be kidding!"

"Oh come on," Dennis said. "Cathy and Emily have done it before. If they can do it, you can do it. Besides, we won't be going very far. Now, take a look at this map, and I'll show you where we're going."

Ted knew the place. He had been there two or three times in the summer. It was a lovely place, with a nice trail going up by a pretty waterfall. Ted had sat by that waterfall to eat his lunch, enjoying its lovely sound. "The waterfall won't be running now, will it?" Ted asked.

"No, of course not. It'll be frozen—a waterfall of ice. We'll camp next to it on the first night." Dennis pointed to the map. "Then we'll go up across this big open meadow and camp again in the woods on the other side. Then, on the third day, if the weather is good, we'll get up to the top," he went on, pointing to a small mountain on the map. "If it's a clear day, we'll be able to see a long way. It'll be really pretty. Then we'll come back down the way we went up."

Ted looked at the map and then at Dennis. "It isn't going to take us five days, is it? I've made it to the top and back down again in two days."

"Sure, it's a two-day hike in the summer. But in the winter it won't seem like the same trail. You'll see."

* * * * *

At 6:00, Ted went back to the girls' apartment for supper. John was already there. "Hi," he said, "I hear you're going with us."

"Yes, I am. I hope I won't mess anything up."

"Oh don't worry, you'll be fine. Dennis says you're a good hiker. I brought your jacket," John went on, holding up a little bag.

"Is it in there?" Ted asked. "I thought it would be bigger than that."

"Watch this!" John said. He opened the bag and started to pull something out. As he pulled on it, it puffed up, getting bigger and bigger, till it was a big, thick jacket. "Try it on," he said.

Ted put it on. He turned around slowly, grinning at the others. "With this and those mittens and those Mickey Mouse boots, I'm going to be too big to move!"

As soon as Dennis got there with the sleeping bag for Ted, they all sat down to eat. They began to talk about other winter trips that they had been on. They all talked at once about things that had happened and places they had been.

Ted began to feel excited. This was the start of something new for him. He could hardly wait for the next day. He wanted to get started!

Later he walked home through the same cold streets. But now he didn't mind the wind, and the snow looked almost pretty to him. He wanted to see lots of it. There would be snow up to his neck, Dennis had said!

Suddenly he stopped in the middle of the sidewalk. Snow up to his neck! That made him think of something, but he couldn't quite remember what. Something about a lot of snow. He couldn't think of it. Oh well, it didn't matter.

When he got back to his apartment, he looked at his backpack leaning against the wall. He picked it up and tried it on. It didn't feel so heavy now. Then he tried on the boots and the snowshoes and walked around and around on his rug. Tomorrow he would be putting them on for real. Tomorrow, he thought. Tomorrow.

* * * * *

Early the next morning, Dennis was at the door. "Ready?" he asked.

"Ready!" Ted said as he grabbed his backpack. Dennis picked up the boots and snowshoes. They were off!

They hurried down the stairs and out to the street, where the others were waiting in Cathy's station wagon. The back of the car was filled almost to the roof. "Can you get your stuff in?" Cathy called.

Ted opened the back of the car, picked up his pack, and pushed it in. Dennis pushed in the snowshoes and boots beside it. "I got you some ski poles to use with the snowshoes," he told Ted.

"OK." Ted slammed down the back of the station wagon and climbed into the back seat. "Let's go!"

The car pulled out into the snowy street. Soon they were out of the city. It was good to be out on the open road again.

It was still a long way to the mountain. They talked and told jokes and sang songs, and the time went by quickly.

Suddenly, bang! The car spun around as Cathy hung onto the wheel, fighting to keep the car on the road. At last it skidded to a stop. "Is everybody all right?" Cathy called.

"Yes, I think so," John said.

"Yes, we're all right," the others said. "What happened?"

"I think we had a blowout," Cathy said as she pulled the car off the road and got out. "Yes, that's what happened—a blowout."

"Do you have a spare tire?" Emily asked.

"Yes, it's right there in the tire well, under all our things."

"Oh, no!" everybody groaned. They all got out and looked at the flat tire, then at all the things in the car. "Oh well, we might as well get to work," John said.

Out came the backpacks, the sleeping bags, and the tents. Out came the snowshoes and the ski poles and the boots. Out came the food, the cooking pots and the little stoves. At last, out came the spare tire.

First John worked on the nuts while Cathy set up the jack. Then they jacked up the car while Ted stood by with the spare tire. As cars passed by on the road, people smiled and waved at them. "I feel like a fool, standing here with all this stuff," Emily said.

"Don't worry, it won't take a minute with all of us working," Ted said.

As soon as John got the flat tire off, Ted lifted up the spare tire and slid it into place. John put on the nuts, then let the jack down. They put the flat tire into the tire well and started to put all their things back into the car. "I've never had a blowout before," Cathy said. "We were lucky we didn't roll the car over."

"What a way to start our trip," Emily said. "I hope it isn't a bad sign."

A bad sign. Ted stopped and looked at her, trying to think. There was something he should remember. Something was going to happen. But what? What?

"Oh, don't talk like that," Dennis was telling Emily. "We had a spare tire, didn't we? And we didn't lose much time at all getting it on. It didn't even take very long to take all our stuff out and put it back in. So don't worry! What else could happen?" He jumped into the car shouting, "Let's go!"

The others got into the car, and Cathy drove back

onto the road. Everything seemed to be fine. Soon they were talking and telling jokes again. But Ted leaned over to talk to Emily. "You don't really believe in bad signs, do you?" he asked.

"No, of course not. I was just being silly. You heard what Dennis said. What else could happen?"

"Look!" Cathy called out as they went around a turn in the road. She was pointing at something far ahead of them.

There in front of them, shining white in the sun, was the mountain.

Comprehension Questions/*Chapter 1*

Directions. Answer these questions about the chapter you have just read. Put an *x* in the box beside the best answer to each question.

1. (D) How did Ted feel when he woke up from his nightmare?

   ☐ a. He was happy that it was over.
   ☐ b. He wanted to go back to sleep.
   ☐ c. He was scared and upset.
   ☐ d. He felt like a fool.

2. (C) What did Dennis do first?

   ☐ a. He took Ted to the camping store.
   ☐ b. He talked Ted into going on the camping trip.
   ☐ c. He had supper at the girls' apartment.
   ☐ d. He helped Ted pack his backpack.

3. (A) Dennis said, "In winter, you have the woods *all to yourself*." What does this mean?

   ☐ a. Ted owns the woods.
   ☐ b. There are no other people in the woods.
   ☐ c. Ted will see every tree.
   ☐ d. Ted must go on the camping trip alone.

4. (B) Who got the food for the trip?

- ☐ a. Cathy
- ☐ b. John
- ☐ c. Ted and Dennis
- ☐ d. Sue and Emily

5. (E) They had to take so many things with them on their winter hiking trip because they

- ☐ a. had to be prepared for the cold.
- ☐ b. were going to be gone for five years.
- ☐ c. thought Ted might lose his things.
- ☐ d. thought that it would keep them from having nightmares.

6. (D) People get frostbite

- ☐ a. every time they go winter camping.
- ☐ b. when they wear too many jackets.
- ☐ c. when they set up their tents.
- ☐ d. when their bodies get too cold.

7. (B) Ted's boots were called Mickey Mouse boots because

- ☐ a. they were big and black like Mickey Mouse's feet.
- ☐ b. they were little, like a mouse's feet.
- ☐ c. they were on the Mickey Mouse show on TV.
- ☐ d. they made people feel silly.

8. (E) How did Ted feel about camping in the winter?

- ☐ a. He didn't like camping at all.
- ☐ b. It was new to him, but he wanted to try it.
- ☐ c. He knew a lot about it, and he wanted to go again.
- ☐ d. He thought it was crazy.

9. (C) What did they do first after the blowout?

- ☐ a. Jacked up the car
- ☐ b. Put on the spare tire
- ☐ c. Took the spare tire out of the car
- ☐ d. Took all their camping things out of the car

10. (A) Emily thought that the tire blowout might be a *bad sign*. What does this mean?

- ☐ a. A road sign saying BAD ROAD AHEAD
- ☐ b. A road sign that had tipped over
- ☐ c. Something showing that bad things were going to happen
- ☐ d. Something showing that they were going to have a good time

Skills Used to Answer Questions

A. Recognizing Words in Context
B. Recalling Facts
C. Keeping Events in Order
D. Making Inferences
E. Understanding the Main Idea

Prefixes

A prefix is a group of letters added to the beginning of a word. A prefix changes the meaning of a word. Here are some common prefixes with their meanings:

Prefix	Meaning
un- →	not
re- →	again
anti- →	against

If you add *un-* to *happy,* you get the word *unhappy.* The prefix *un-* means *not.* So *unhappy* means *not happy.*

The prefix *re-* means *again.* If you add *re-* to *write,* you get the word *rewrite. Rewrite* means *write again.*

The prefix *anti-* means *against.* If you add *anti-* to *rust,* you get the word *antirust. Antirust* means *against rust.*

Adding prefixes to these words changed their meanings. You can see that adding a prefix makes a new word with a new meaning. Here are some other common prefixes and their meanings:

Prefix	Meaning	Example
pre- →	before →	preheat
mis- →	wrong →	misread
inter- →	between →	interstate

Exercise 1

Each word below has a prefix. Underline the prefix in each word. Then print the prefix on the line below the word. Remember that a prefix is a group of letters added to the beginning of a word. The first one has been done for you.

1. <u>inter</u>national	4. misunderstand	7. mistreat
inter ______	______	______
2. untied	5. rethink	8. pregame
______	______	______
3. prepay	6. untested	9. replay
______	______	______

Exercise 2

Each sentence below has a word with a prefix. Find the word with the prefix and print it on the line below the sentence. Then circle the prefix. The first one has been done for you.

1. Sam was unsure about where to go.

   (un)sure ______________________

2. When winter comes, you must put antifreeze in your car.

   ____

3. If you miss a TV show tonight, you can see a rerun of the same show tomorrow.

____

4. Prewashed fruit can be eaten right from the box.

____

5. The bridge looked unsafe.

____

6. Our team played in the intercity match.

____

7. Maria hurt herself when her gun misfired.

____

Exercise 3

Below, each word on the left has a prefix. The list on the right shows word meanings. Find the meaning on the right that goes best with each word on the left. Use the boxes that show prefixes and their meanings at the beginning of the lesson to help you. Print the meaning on the line next to the word. The first one has been done for you.

1. <u>pre</u>war	before war	use wrong
2. <u>re</u>heat	______________	use again
3. <u>mis</u>use	______________	before war

4. antiwar ________________ heat again

5. reuse ________________ heat before

6. preheat ________________ against war

Local Phone Numbers

You probably use the telephone every day. Most of the time, you telephone people in your town or city. The area around your own town or city is called the *local area.* When you call someone in this area, you are making a *local call.*

To make a local call, you must use a phone number. A local phone number looks like this: 421-8162. You can find local phone numbers in the *telephone book.* The telephone book will have numbers for people and for businesses.

Here is part of a page from a phone book:

Ancone Linda 146 Russell St Brgfld **723-6418**
Anderson Arthur E 31 General St Bngr **332-9216**
Anderson Arthur P 183 Manson Ave Dumnt ... **384-3364**
Anderson J 82 Sunny Cove Dr Scit **749-1351**
Anderson M 22 Garfield Av Tnck **721-1983**
Andrade Esther 334 Dionne St Montvl **529-4427**
Barber CA 5 Red St Lewstn **461-1179**
Bennett John N 57 Pembroke Dr Brkln **739-2527**
Cardoso Jose 268 Florence Rd Upton **863-6942**

Each line in the phone book tells you three things. It tells you a person's *name.* It tells you a person's *address.* It tells you a person's *phone number.* Here is what one line looks like:

last name	first name	middle initial	street address	town or city	phone number
Bennett	**John**	**N**	57 Pembroke Dr	Brkln	739-2527

Shortened Words

You can see that some of the words in this line from the phone book have letters left out. The letters are left out to make the words shorter. This is done so that more words can fit on a page.

Look at these words from the listing: **Dr** and **Brkln**. These words have letters left out. The whole words are **Drive** and **Brooklyn**.

Most phone listings use shortened words for the street address. Some common shortened words are:

St for Street
Dr for Drive
Av for Avenue
Rd for Road

The phone book also uses shortened words for towns and cities. Try to learn the shortened words for the towns and cities in your local area.

1. Look at the sixth name in the list of telephone numbers. What is the person's first name?

____

2. Where does she live? Copy the address here.

____

3. What is her telephone number?

____

Alphabetical Order

In a phone book, names are listed in *alphabetical order.* That means that names are placed in order according to the letters of the alphabet that they begin with. Look at the list of names from the phone book at the beginning of the lesson. You can see that names that begin with *A* are at the beginning of the list. Names that begin with *B* come next, and so on.

When many names begin with the same letter, they are put in order according to their second letters. If the second letters are the same, they are put in order according to their third letters, and so on. *Barber* comes before *Bennett* on the list. That is because *a* comes before *e* in the alphabet.

Sometimes two or more people have the same last name. Then the first name is used to put their names in alphabetical order. Sometimes both the first and the last names are the same. Then the middle name is used to put the names in alphabetical order.

4. Look at the first two names in the list of phone numbers. Print those names on the lines below. Then, in each name, circle the letter that was used to put the names in alphabetical order.

____

____

5. Look at the list again. Which name comes first, *Anderson M* or *Anderson J?* Print the name that comes first.

____

6. If there was a listing for *Anderson B,* would it come before *Anderson J* or after *Anderson J?* Circle your answer.

before **after**

Finding Local Phone Numbers

A telephone book lists the names of people who have telephones. You know that the names are listed in alphabetical order. The address and phone number of each person are also given. Below is part of a page taken from a telephone book:

DIX—DOIRON

Dix E 120 Warren Av E Prv	438-5457
Dix H A 3663 Pawt Av E Prv	433-3289
Dix Jas C 312 Dover Av E Prv	438-6226
Dix Jos I 197 Don Av E Prv	434-3073
Dix Ronald C 12 Mathurin Rd Plainvil	695-0009
Dix Wm H Jr 156 Putnam E Prv	434-8736
Dixelle Co jwlry 31 Privet Pawt	728-7500
Dixie's Paint & Hardware 2260 W Shore Rd Wrwk	737-0977
Dixie's Radio & TV 2260 W Shore Rd Wrwk	737-0977
DIXON --- See also Dickson	
Dixon Beulah B Mrs 114 California Av Prov	941-1105
Dixon Candis 226 Gano Prov	273-6284
Dixon Chas E 182 Sabin Pawt	724-8091
Dixon Chas E Jr 91 Mooreland Av Crns	781-2169
Dixon Cornelius Sr 19 Bain Crns	942-6368
Dixon Corp plstc 386 Metacom Av Bris	253-2000
Dixon David R 16 Carson Pawt	728-8322
Dixon Donald R 81 Angell Av Crns	944-0789
Dixon E M 1214 Cranston Crns	943-3740
Dixon Edw W 82 Fairvw Av Cmb	723-8143
Dixon F 27 Phillips Cov	822-2026
Dixon Geo Jr 82 Lindy Av E Prv	433-2463
Dixon Geo O 12 Ballou Av Lcln	723-0685
Dixon & Hayes Inc Windsor Rd Fos	647-2755
Dixon Herman 88 Doyle Av Prov	421-0027
Dixon Inc 386 Metacom Av Bris	253-2000
Dixon J Leonard 111 Wannamoistt Rd E Prv	438-5049
Dixon Jas 295 Mendon Av Pawt	725-6105
Dixon Jas B 24 Whitfrd Av Pawt	728-4364
Dixon Kenneth 144 Hopkins Hl Rd Cov	821-1456
Dixon Kevin J Victory Hwy Exetr	397-3292
Dixon M A 273 Chatham Cir Wrwk	738-3453
Dixon Margaret M 57 Weedn Av E Prv	434-4681
Dixon Oliver 2260 W Shore Rd Wrwk	737-0977
Res 14 Hillcrst Av Wrwk	737-6648
Dixon Paul 1022 Hope Prov	751-8260
Dixon R 38 Read Av Cov	822-1627
Dixon Richard C 8 Betty Lcln	724-7747
Dixon Richard J 56 Friendly Rd E Grn	884-4585
Dixon Robt E Jr 34 Ballou Cmb	765-0241
Dixon Russell E 172 Kimbll Prov	831-0684
Dixon S E 1 Jackson Wlkwy Prov	274-8257
Dixon T A 24 Whitfrd Av Pawt	728-4364
Dixon Thos 7 Bellvu Blvd E Prv	434-8496
Dobbins Lynne F Peeptoad Rd N Scit	934-0682
Dobbins Mark 120 Cindy-Ann Dr E Grn	884-9430
Dobbins Richard A 11 Presidnt Av Prov	351-0742
Dobbins Robt C 107 Young Pawt	722-8149
Dobbs Elwood D 50 Arnold Rd Cov	826-0431
Dobbyn Dennis M & Barbara 7 Almeida Dr Wrn	245-1356
Dobek Edw N 30 Rosewd Av S Attl	761-7110
Dobek L L 50 Murray Cov	828-4925
Dobek Theodore E 106 Garfld C F	723-5456
Dober Eric W 188 Bay View Av Bris	253-9263
Dobie Dianne 247 Park N Att	699-7806
Dobish C W 57 Alexndr N Prv	353-2106
Doble Guy W 228 Arnold Rd N Att	695-1723
Dobos Frank 22 Casprsn N Kgtwn	884-8590
Dobosz Chas 41 Landgon Av Pawt	724-7597
Dobosz Charlie 111 Suflk Av Pawt	722-9439
Dobosz Jos 21 Briarwd Dr Cmb	728-8631
Dobosz Marion 8 Chunga Dr Cmb	728-0269
Dobosz Michael 689 High C F	726-4345
Dobosz Paul 727 Roosvlt Av Pawt	725-4699
Doboszynski Jos C 119 Cottge Av N Prv	353-2484
Doboszynski Wm 147 Dover Prov	831-2682
Dobras Felix 74 Met Pk Av Seek	761-7536
Dobras Ferdinand A 126 Brown Av Seek	761-7516
Dobridnia Leon F 13 Fort Hl Rd Bris	253-8883
Dobrin Richard C 70 Hazltn Crns	942-0896
Dobro David 97 Sutherland Rd N Att	695-1533
Dobrolet Afanasy 15 Mavis Pawt	725-5781
Dobrolet Luba 28 Darrow Pawt	724-4981
Dobrolet Michael 81 Met Av Crns	942-2039
Dobrowolski Jas T & Jeanne M 2587 Division E Grn	885-1713
Dobrowski John 119 Plesnt Plainvil	695-6314
Dobrushkin Boris 235 Baker Prov	941-3879
Dobrushkin Boris 123 Burlington Prov	351-6906
Dobrzynski Robt J phys 200 Toll Gt Rd Wrwk	737-5253
Dobson Agnes 52 Ferncrst Blvd N Prv	353-3917
Dobson C 19 Shippee Av W Wrwk	828-2595
Dobson Chas 44 Colvintown Rd Cov	822-0092
Dobson Co 1199 Eddy Prov	461-5244
Dobson Donald Mrs 25 Dean Av Jstn	231-6558
Dobson John Mrs 120 Putnam Av Jstn	231-9154
Dobson L 33 Washngtn C F	723-8597
Dobson M G 9 Parkis Av Prov	351-8471
Dobson Robt J & Janet Cranberry Rd N Att	695-0049
DOBY CORP 715 Putnam Pke Grnvl	949-0220
Doby Geo 158 Custer Wrwk	738-8720

Exercise 1

Look at the page from the phone book. Find the phone numbers for the people listed below. Remember that last names are in alphabetical order. The first one has been done for you.

1. Frank Dobos 884-8590
2. Donald Dixon ______________
3. Ronald C Dix ______________
4. Dianne Dobie ______________

Exercise 2

Use the page from the phone book to find the addresses of the people listed below. Copy the address for each from the phone book. The first one has been done for you.

1. Dixelle Co 31 Privet Pawt
2. Elwood D Dobbs ______________
3. Lynne F Dobbins ______________
4. Herman Dixon ______________

Exercise 3

Use the page from the phone book to answer the questions below. Find the information you need. Then print your answers on the lines. The first one has been done for you.

1. On what street does Guy W Doble live?

   Arnold Rd

2. What is the phone number of Mrs. Beulah B Dixon?

   ____

3. In what town does Michael Dobrolet live?

   ____

4. What is the complete address of L L Dobek?

   ____

2

Buried Alive!

Preview Words/*Chapter 2*

Study the words in the box. Then read the sentences below with your teacher. Look carefully at the words in boldface type.

body	easier	numb	spread
breathing	follow	ourselves	steadily
buried	freeze	pictures	stumbled
chocolate	listened	piece	thrashed
covered	marked	prettier	voice

1. We have the mountain to **ourselves**.
2. Your clothes would get wet. Then they would **freeze**.
3. He **stumbled** and almost fell.
4. He was **covered** with snow from head to foot.
5. Emily was eating a **chocolate** bar.
6. Ted stayed at the end where it was **easier** to walk.
7. Emily took some **pictures**.
8. They walked up between the trees, slowly and **steadily**.
9. Ted took a **piece** of cheese out of the bag.
10. The trail is **marked**.
11. Let's **spread** out and see if we can find it.
12. He **listened**, but he couldn't hear the others.
13. He was **buried** under the snow!
14. Ted **thrashed** around with his arms.
15. They would **follow** his tracks.
16. His hands were starting to get **numb**.
17. They would take his frozen **body** down the mountain.
18. "Don't worry," a **voice** said.
19. The woods looked **prettier** than ever.
20. All he could hear was the others **breathing**.

When they pulled into a parking lot by the side of the road, there were no other cars around. "Oh good," said Dennis, "we have the mountain to ourselves. What a day! And what a trip this is going to be!"

"I just hope the weather holds," Emily said.

"Worry, worry, worry! All you ever do is worry," Dennis told her. "Look at that sun! Look at that blue sky! What more could you ask for? Come on, let's get those packs on and hit that trail!"

Once more they took all their things out of the car. While Cathy split up the food to put in their packs, Dennis showed Ted how to strap the sleeping bag onto his pack. The others were busy putting on their boots and then their snowshoes.

Suddenly Ted saw that the others were taking off their big jackets and putting them into their packs. "Why are they doing that?" he asked Dennis. "It's *cold* out here!"

"You won't feel cold when you get moving," Dennis told him. "You would get too hot if you hiked in your jacket. Then you would sweat, and your clothes would get wet. Later they would freeze. And if your clothes freeze, they can't keep you warm."

Ted heard John call out, "I'll start to break the trail." The others were leaving already! Quickly, Ted finished putting on his snowshoes, then took off his jacket and stuffed it into his pack. When he lifted his heavy pack up onto his back, he almost groaned out loud. He had never carried this much before, and he had sure never carried it on snowshoes!

John turned and walked into the woods, followed by

Cathy and then Emily. They were gone, with nothing left to show where they had gone but their snowshoe tracks.

Ted tried to hurry after them, but after two steps he stumbled and almost fell under the heavy pack. There was so much about winter camping that he didn't know. Would he do the right things? Could he keep up with the others? Or would he make a fool of himself? Maybe he shouldn't have let Dennis push him into this.

The next five days were going to be long ones.

Ted stumbled along the trail of snowshoe tracks. His snowshoes sank into the soft snow, but they didn't hit the ground. How deep was the snow?

It was hard to walk in the snowshoes. Ted's feet felt so wide and heavy, and he had to walk with his feet wide apart. Suddenly he stepped down with one snowshoe on top of the other one and fell flat on his face in the snow.

The heavy pack was on top of him, holding him down. He couldn't move.

There he was, lying on his face in the snow with seventy pounds on top of him and two great big things tied to his feet. He had left the nice, warm city streets for *this?*

Dennis came up behind him and asked, "What happened to you?"

"I stepped on my own big feet," Ted said. "I can't get up."

"Roll over on your side," Dennis said. "Now sit up. That's right. Now stand up. See? What's so hard about that?"

Ted looked down at himself. He was covered with snow from head to foot. "Brush yourself off," Dennis told him. "You can't let that snow melt on you. It would get your clothes wet, and—"

"I know, I know," Ted cut in. "And my clothes would freeze. And if my clothes freeze, they can't keep me warm." He brushed himself off carefully.

Dennis brushed off Ted's pack, then gave Ted a pair of ski poles. "Here, you went off without these," he said. "They'll help to hold you up. Why were you trying to go so fast, anyway?"

"I was trying to catch up with the others," Ted said.

"They'll wait for you. After all, we can't go any faster than the slowest person."

The slowest person! That hurt. Ted turned and walked up the trail.

He walked for only a minute or two before he found the others waiting by a big pine tree. Emily had stuck her ski poles into the snow and hung her mittens on them so that she could eat a chocolate bar. She smiled at Ted as he came up and asked, "Would you like some chocolate? It will give you some pep."

"I'm fine, thanks," Ted said crossly. Emily smiled and tucked the chocolate bar into Ted's front pocket. John swung around and started to walk into the smooth, deep snow.

It was easier now for Ted to keep up. The person in front, breaking the trail, sank deep into the snow at every step. It was slow, tiring work, and everybody but Ted took turns. Ted stayed at the end of the line where it was easier to walk.

Soon, as the snowshoes began to feel good on his feet, Ted began to look around him. The woods *were* lovely. The sun shone between the trees, shining brightly on each branch. Sometimes the wind would blow softly, and snow would blow off the branches and fall slowly to the ground, sparkling in the sun.

"Look!" said John, pointing at a line of tiny footprints going off into the woods. "A rabbit came through here."

They stopped for a minute while Emily took some pictures. Cathy took off her pack, got out some little bags, and handed one to each person. "Your lunch," she told Ted.

Ted looked at the bag. It held bits of chocolate, some cheese, nuts, and a few crackers. "This is lunch?" he asked.

"Have you ever eaten a frozen sandwich?" Cathy asked. "This won't freeze. Also, we can't stop to eat because we'd get cold."

They moved on up between the trees, slowly and steadily. Ted took a piece of cheese out of the bag and put the bag in his pocket. He walked along eating the cheese and looking around him. This was the life.

Now Emily was in front breaking the trail. Suddenly

she stopped and waited till John and Cathy came up to her. They stood talking and pointing up the mountain.

When Ted came up to them he asked, "What's up?"

"We've lost the trail," Emily said.

"But the trail is marked, isn't it?" Ted asked. "There are markers on the trees."

"Yes, but the markers are under the snow, so we can't tell where the trail goes from here. Let's spread out and see if we can find it." They took off their packs and put them in a pile on the snow. People began to move off on each side.

"Be careful," Cathy told Ted. "Don't go too far."

"Don't worry," Ted said. He looked around till he saw a gap in the trees. Maybe the trail went up that way. He set off up the mountain, walking along through the deep snow. He felt very happy. It felt good to take his pack off, but it felt even better to walk on the clean, smooth snow where no one had ever walked before.

He walked along happily, watching his snowshoes sink into the snow or looking around at the snowy woods. He leaned on his ski poles and watched a little bird hop from branch to branch of a tree. He forgot all about looking for the trail. He forgot about how far away he was from the others.

Suddenly he remembered. He stopped still and listened, but he couldn't hear the others walking or talking. It was very quiet. There was no sound but the little bird singing in the tree. Ted felt very alone.

He looked back along his snowshoe track bending this way and that way through the snow. "I'll just take a quick look around for that trail," Ted thought. "Then I'd better get back to the others. They must have found the trail by now anyway."

Ted looked around. Near him there was a tiny hill,

not much more than a bump in the snow. "If I get up on that," he thought, "maybe I'll see something. Then I'll go back." He walked over to the bump in the snow and put one snowshoe up on it. In a flash, a pine tree sprang up under his feet. Ted felt himself falling! Down, down he went, feet first, right down into the snow. Soft snow fell down all around him and on top of him. He was buried under the snow!

Ted thrashed around with his arms, but he could hardly move. He tried to shout, but the snow cut off his voice. All around him was a cold, white world.

He had to climb out of here! He tried to push with his snowshoes, but now they held him down. He couldn't move his feet at all. He pulled at the snow with his hands, but it just slid down around him. He couldn't lift himself up unless he had something to push on. He tried to pack the snow down around him, but it was so soft and loose, it just wouldn't pack down.

Why did this have to happen? How could he have been such a fool? Why had he gone so far away from the others? Why? Why? He beat at the snow with his hands and shouted, "Hey! Get me out of here!"

Suddenly more snow fell onto his face. The snow around him was moving! It was coming down on him! It filled in all the space around his head. He could feel it pushing up against his face. He was being buried deeper and deeper!

He must hold still! He must not move or he would shake more snow down on himself. He must stay quiet!

The others would find him, wouldn't they? They would find out that he had gone off by himself, and follow his tracks. All he had to do was wait.

He waited.

He tried to hold still. Every time he moved, more

snow came down on him. But it didn't take long for him to start getting cold. Very cold.

He could hardly feel his feet. Even his hands were starting to get numb. The snow stung his bare face and ears. He thought about the jacket in his pack. Why had he taken it off?

How long would it take him to freeze to death?

He thought about his friends taking his frozen body down the mountain. Or maybe they wouldn't find him at all. Maybe they wouldn't find him till the snow melted in the spring.

Suddenly he felt the snow above him shaking. "Don't worry," a voice said, "we'll get you out!" It was Dennis! He was saved!

The snow above him began to move. A moment later, the end of a snowshoe stuck down over his head. Then sunlight, as a hole broke open above him. He could see Dennis's face looking down at him.

"I'll have you out of there in a minute!" Dennis said, digging quickly with his snowshoe. The hole above Ted got bigger and bigger. Now he could see Cathy and John reaching down to him. He grabbed their hands, and they tried to pull him up.

He didn't move.

"Kick your feet!" Cathy said. "Try to tip up your snowshoes, they're holding you down."

Ted pulled up on his toes, straining against the snowshoes, till he could feel them begin to move. "I'm getting it!" he said.

"OK, everyone," Cathy said, "one . . . two . . . three . . . *pull!*" They all pulled at once. Suddenly the snow gave way and Ted popped up. He found himself lying most of the way out of the hole. He could feel snow falling down all around him into the hole.

John helped him pull himself the rest of the way out of the hole. Ted stood up carefully and turned around slowly, looking at the woods around him. Wow, it was great to be out of that hole. The woods looked prettier than ever. Then he turned to Dennis and asked, "How did you find me?"

"Well, we were looking for you," Dennis said. "We were following your tracks. But when we got here, your tracks just stopped. We thought you had turned around and gone back the way you had come. We almost turned around, too! But then we saw your ski pole sticking out of the snow."

He gave the ski pole to Ted. Ted looked down at it, laying across his hand. He had come so close.

"But what happened to me?" Ted asked. "Where did that hole come from? I was just walking up this little hill, and—"

"Little hill?" Dennis asked with a crooked smile. "That will do it every time. There's your little hill," he said, pointing at a big pine tree near them. It looked funny in the snowy woods because there was almost no snow on it.

"That's my hill? What do you mean?" Ted asked.

"That tree was bent over by the snow. More and more snow fell on it, holding it down. But when you stepped on it, you let it go. It popped up, and you fell into the hole in the snow where it had been."

"But . . . but . . . the snow was so *deep!* My feet never even hit the ground!" Ted said.

"What did I tell you?" Dennis smiled. "Snow up to your neck. But I didn't know that you were going to try it out."

"Come on!" Cathy called. "Ted is cold! Let's get

moving! Ted, don't forget to brush yourself off. If your clothes get wet—"

"I know, I know—if my clothes get wet, they'll freeze. Just give me a minute." Ted brushed himself off quickly, then walked back down along the track he had made. The others followed close behind him.

When they got back to where they had left their packs, Emily was waiting for them, walking up and down. She had her jacket on. That looked good! Ted grabbed his pack and got out his jacket and his hat.

"Are you all right, Ted?" Emily asked. "We were so worried!"

"Next time, don't get so far away from us!" Cathy said. "You're new at this, and you never know when you'll need our help. I can't believe how lucky you were this time. You—"

"Thank you for coming to help me," Ted cut in. "By the way, did you find the trail?"

"Yes, we did," John said. "We go up over there."

Ted grabbed his pack, put it on, and said, "So let's go!"

* * * * *

The afternoon went by. Now, as the sun sank lower, long shadows lay across the snow.

Ted was getting very tired. This was much more work than hiking in the summer! It would be dark soon. How much longer would it take them to get to the waterfall where they were going to camp? Ted wished that he could ask Dennis, but he was afraid that Cathy would hear him. He just kept going.

At last they came around some pine trees, and there it was! The waterfall! It was so pretty that Ted stopped short in the middle of the trail. The waterfall seemed to be hanging in the air, ice piled up in wave after wave. It sparkled all different colors in the setting sun. The waterfall looks as if it just stopped! Ted said to himself. The way it sparkles! And it seems even more strange that it doesn't make any sound. Winter is a whole new world for me!

"Come on, everyone!" Cathy's voice cut across his thoughts. "We don't have time to stand around. We have to get our camp set up fast. We lost a lot of time back there, looking for Ted . . . I mean, looking for the trail."

Yes, boss, Ted said to himself as he turned away from the waterfall and walked over to the others.

"Take all the food out of your packs and put it right here," Cathy was saying. "Dennis, will you show Ted how to set up his tent? Emily, you have the other tent, don't you? John, why don't you get the stoves set up? Now, for supper we're having stew. Who has the bag with the stew in it? Someone should get some water—there's a little bit of water dripping off the waterfall. John, will you get the water? Now—"

Her voice went on and on. Ted was glad he had to set up his tent, just to get away from her. After Dennis showed him how to stamp down the snow with his snowshoes, the tent went up quickly. They tied it to some trees to help hold it up.

By the time they were done, it was dark. Supper was cooking. Everything was quiet. Ted felt very tired, but happy. And supper smelled good!

John was stirring the stew. He stopped stirring and looked into the pot with a flashlight. "There's too much steam, I can't see a thing! I'll just have to try it," he said as he put the spoon into his mouth. "It's getting there. Maybe I should try it one more time." He started to put the spoon back into the stew.

"Hey, save some for the rest of us," Dennis called.

"The stew is ready. Get your cups," John called. Quickly everyone crowded around him, and he spooned the hot stew into their cups. As soon as his cup was filled, Ted dug right in. He had never been so hungry!

He stood next to his tent, spooning down his stew. Suddenly he slipped and some of the stew spilled onto the tent. "Rats!" Ted said, looking around for something to clean up the spilled stew with. He rubbed at it with his mitten, but already the stew was frozen hard.

Ted looked at the frozen stew. He looked around at the winter woods. He looked up at the sky, at the stars. They looked very cold and far away.

How cold *was* it out here? What if the others hadn't found him this afternoon? What if he were still back there in that hole, under the snow? Ted dug into his stew again.

They ate stew and more stew, then ended up with hot chocolate. When they couldn't hold anymore, they put their things in the tents. Soon they were in their sleeping bags.

It was still early. They talked for a while, but one by one the voices stopped. Soon everyone was asleep but Ted. He lay there thinking and listening to the breathing of the others and the wind in the trees. It was so quiet, so peaceful, that Ted didn't want to go to sleep. He didn't want to miss a minute of it. He . . .

Ted was asleep.

Comprehension Questions/*Chapter 2*

Directions. Answer these questions about the chapter you have just read. Put an *x* in the box beside the best answer to each question.

1. (D) What did Ted think about Cathy?

☐ a. He thought she was fun to be with.
☐ b. He thought she was bossy.
☐ c. He thought she knew a lot about camping.
☐ d. He thought she was in love with Dennis.

2. (C) Which of these things happened last?

☐ a. Ted stepped on his own snowshoe.
☐ b. Ted fell down and couldn't get up.
☐ c. Dennis showed Ted how to put his sleeping bag on his pack.
☐ d. Ted tried to catch up with the others.

3. (B) Why did Ted have to brush the snow off his clothes?

☐ a. So that no one would know he fell down
☐ b. So the snow wouldn't get in his way
☐ c. Because he didn't like the way it looked
☐ d. So that his clothes wouldn't get wet and freeze

4. (A) Emily said, "Let's *spread out* and look for the trail." What does this mean?

- ☐ a. Lie down in the snow
- ☐ b. Lay out our camping things
- ☐ c. Each go a different way
- ☐ d. Sit down and eat lunch

5. (C) Which of these things happened first?

- ☐ a. Ted fell into a hole.
- ☐ b. Ted stepped on a tree that was bent down by the snow.
- ☐ c. Ted went off by himself to look for the trail.
- ☐ d. Ted yelled for help.

6. (A) "*In a flash,* the pine tree sprang up under Ted's feet." What does this mean?

- ☐ a. With a bright light
- ☐ b. Very quickly
- ☐ c. Inside a flashlight
- ☐ d. With a new thought

7. (B) How did the others find Ted after they followed his tracks?

- ☐ a. They saw his ski pole sticking out of the snow.
- ☐ b. He called for help.
- ☐ c. They saw the snow moving over him.
- ☐ d. They waited for him to come back.

8. (D) Why did Cathy tell everyone how to set up the camp?

- ☐ a. She was the only one who had ever been camping before.
- ☐ b. The others kept asking her how to do it.
- ☐ c. She was the kind of person who likes to tell everyone what to do.
- ☐ d. She was the only one who had ever set up a tent.

9. (E) What is the main thing that happened to Ted in this part of the story?

- ☐ a. He got buried under the snow.
- ☐ b. He lost his ski pole.
- ☐ c. He lost the trail.
- ☐ d. He fell down on his snowshoes.

10. (E) What is the main thing that Ted found out on the first day of the trip?

- ☐ a. Dennis was not his friend after all.
- ☐ b. Chocolate bars will give you pep.
- ☐ c. The snow really was up to his chin.
- ☐ d. Winter hiking can be full of danger.

Skills Used to Answer Questions

A. Recognizing Words in Context
B. Recalling Facts
C. Keeping Events in Order
D. Making Inferences
E. Understanding Main Ideas

Using Prefixes to Learn New Words

You know that a prefix is a group of letters added to the beginning of a word. A prefix changes the meaning of a word. In the last chapter, you learned some common prefixes and their meanings. Review those prefixes and their meanings in the box below.

Prefix	Meaning	Example
un- →	not →	unhappy
re- →	again →	rewrite
anti- →	against →	antirust
pre- →	before →	preheat
mis- →	wrong →	misread
inter- →	between →	interstate

Here are some more common prefixes and their meanings:

Prefix	Meaning	Example
non- →	not →	nonstop
sub- →	under, below →	submarine
semi- →	half →	semiprivate
dis- →	not →	dishonest

Knowing a few common prefixes will help you understand words you might not know already.

To understand a word with a prefix, follow these steps:

1. Find the prefix.
2. Separate the prefix from the word it is added to.
3. Look at the two parts. See if you know what either part means.
4. Figure out what the word and the prefix mean together.

For example, maybe you don't know the word *unhurt*. But you can see it has the prefix *un-*. Separate *unhurt* into *un-* and *hurt*. Now you can figure out what the word means. You know that *hurt* means *harmed*. You know that *un-* means *not*. So you can guess that *unhurt* means *not harmed* or *not hurt*.

Pleasant means *nice*. What does *unpleasant* mean?

___

Semi- is a prefix that means *half*. What does *semicircle* mean?

___

Say you see the word *disorganized* and you don't know what it means. But you know the prefix *dis-*. Break the word into two parts: *dis-* and *organized*. You can figure out that this word means *not organized*. You can do the same thing with the word *displeased*. Break it into *dis-* and *pleased*. Then you can see that it means *not pleased*.

Exercise 1

Each word in this exercise has a prefix. Begin by breaking the word into its two parts. Write the prefix first, and then the word. Then print the meaning of the word on the last line. Use these steps to help you:

1. Find the prefix.
2. Separate the prefix from the word it is added to.
3. Print the prefix and the word it has been added to on the lines provided.
4. Figure out what the prefix and the word mean together. Print the meaning on the line provided. Use the prefixes and meanings in the boxes at the beginning of this lesson to help you.

The first one has been done for you.

Word with Prefix	Prefix	Word	Meaning of Word with Prefix
1. semiformal	semi	formal	half formal
2. untidy			
3. misunderstand			
4. preview			
5. subhuman			
6. nonsense			
7. interchange			

Exercise 2

Below is another list of words with prefixes. Print the meaning of each word on the line next to the word. Use the steps for understanding a word with a prefix on page 63. The first one has been done for you.

1. disordered not ordered
2. relight ______
3. semisweet ______
4. mistreat ______
5. nonworker ______
6. dishonest ______
7. anticancer ______

Long Distance Phone Calls

The phone book lists the names, addresses and phone numbers of people who have telephones. All the people listed in any phone book live in the same area. This is called the *local area.* All phone calls made to people in this area are called *local phone calls.* To make a local phone call, you dial the phone number listed in the phone book.

Sometimes you want to make a phone call to someone who doesn't live in your local area. This is called a *long distance phone call.* To make a long distance phone call, you need to know more than the person's local phone number. You also need to know the *area code.* An area code is three numbers that go in front of the local phone number when you make a long distance call. The area code tells what area of the country you are calling.

Finding an Area Code

Suppose you want to make a long distance phone call. You know the local number you want to call, but you do not know the area code. You can find the area code by looking in your phone book. The phone book gives a list of area codes. It looks like this:

LONG DISTANCE CALLING

area codes for some cities

place	area code
ALABAMA	
All Points	205
ALASKA	
All Points	907
ARIZONA	
All Points	602
ARKANSAS	
All Points	501
CALIFORNIA	
Anaheim	714
Bakersfield	805
Fresno	209
Los Angeles	213
Oakland	415
Sacramento	916
San Diego	714
San Francisco	415
San Jose	408
Santa Rosa	707
COLORADO	
All Points	303
CONNECTICUT	
All Points	203
DELAWARE	
All Points	302
INDIANA	
Gary	219
Hammond	219
Indianapolis	317
South Bend	219
IOWA	
Cedar Rapids	319
Davenport	319
Des Moines	515
Sioux City	712
KANSAS	
Kansas City	913
Topeka	913
Wichita	316
KENTUCKY	
Covington	606
Frankfort	502
Louisville	502
LOUISIANA	
Baton Rouge	504
New Orleans	504
Shreveport	318
MAINE	
All Points	207
MARYLAND	
All points	301
NEW YORK	
Albany	518
Bay Shore	516
Binghamton	607
Brooklyn	212
Buffalo	716
Mount Vernon	914
New Rochelle	914
New York City	212
Niagara Falls	716
Poughkeepsie	914
Rochester	716
Rome	315
Schenectady	518
Syracuse	315
Tonawanda	716
Troy	518
Utica	315
White Plains	914
Yonkers	914
NORTH CAROLINA	
Asheville	704
Charlotte	704
Durham	919
Greensboro	919
Raleigh	919
Wilmington	919
Winston-Salem	919
NORTH DAKOTA	
All Points	701

To find the area code you want, follow these steps:

1. Find the name of the state you want to call. The states are in alphabetical order.
2. Check to see how many area codes there are in the state. If there is only one area code, you will see the words *all points*. That means that all the numbers in that state have the same area code. For example, all the numbers in Delaware have the same area code: 302.
3. Some states have more than one area code. Then you must look for the name of the city you want to call. If the name of that city is not listed, look for the name of a city near it. The cities are listed in alphabetical order. Use the area code printed next to the city you want. For example, if you wanted to call a city near Bay Shore in New York, you would use the area code 516.

1. To call someone in Maryland, what area code would you use?

____

2. Find New York on the list of area codes. Suppose you want to call someone who lives near Buffalo, New York. Find the area code for Buffalo, New York. What is it?

____

3. What area code would you use to call Albany, New York?

____

Sometimes you may not be able to find the area code you need. Then you can call the operator. The operator will give you the right area code. You call the operator by dialing *0*.

When you have the area code and the phone number, you are ready to make a long distance call.

To make a long distance phone call, you should dial:
1 + the area code + the phone number

For example, to call a person with the area code 516 and the phone number 864-1032, you dial:

1 + 516 + 864-1032

3. What would you dial to call a person with the area code 617 and the phone number 965-1584?

____

Making Long Distance Calls

You know that you have to find the area code before you can make a long distance phone call. You can find an area code by looking at the list of area codes in the phone book. The list is at the beginning of the phone book. Here is part of the list of area codes:

place	area code
ALABAMA	
All Points	205
ALASKA	
All Points	907
ARIZONA	
All Points	602
ARKANSAS	
All Points	501
CALIFORNIA	
Anaheim	714
Bakersfield	805
Fresno	209
Los Angeles	213
Oakland	415
Sacramento	916
San Diego	714
San Francisco	415
San Jose	408
Santa Rosa	707
MICHIGAN	
Dearborn	313
Detroit	313
Escanaba	906
Flint	313
Grand Rapids	616
Lansing	517
Saginaw	517
MINNESOTA	
Duluth	218
Minneapolis	612
Rochester	507
St. Paul	612
MISSISSIPPI	
All Points	601
MISSOURI	
Kansas City	816
St. Louis	314
Springfield	417
MONTANA	
All Points	406
NEBRASKA	
Grand Island	308
Lincoln	402
Omaha	402
NEVADA	
All Points	702
NEW HAMPSHIRE	
All Points	603
NEW JERSEY	
Atlantic City	609
Bayonne	201
Camden	609
Clifton	201
Elizabeth	201
Jersey City	201
Newark	201
Orange	201
Paterson	201
Trenton	609
Woodbridge	201
NEW YORK	
Albany	518
Bay Shore	516
Binghamton	607
Brooklyn	212
Buffalo	716
Mount Vernon	914
New Rochelle	914
New York City	212
Niagara Falls	716
Poughkeepsie	914
Rochester	716
Rome	315
Schenectady	518
Syracuse	315
Tonawanda	716
Troy	518
Utica	315
White Plains	914
Yonkers	914
OKLAHOMA	
Oklahoma City	405
Tulsa	918
VIRGINIA	
Amherst	804
Arlington	703
Harrisonburg	703
Norfolk	804
Richmond	804
Roanoke	703
NEW MEXICO	
All Points	505

Exercise 1

Use the list of area codes to find the area code for each of these cities. Write the area code on the line next to the city. The first one has been done for you.

1. Dearborn, Michigan 313
2. Reno, Nevada ____________________
3. Tulsa, Oklahoma ____________________
4. Jackson, Mississippi ____________________
5. Oakland, California ____________________

Exercise 2

Remember that to make a long distance phone call you must:

1. Find the area code.
2. Dial *1 + the area code + the phone number.*

Write down the numbers you would dial in each case below. The first one has been done for you.

1. You want to call someone in Biloxi, Mississippi. The local number is 468-4542. What will you dial?

   1 + 601 + 468-4542

2. You want to call someone in Rome, New York. The local number is 683-6495. What will you dial?

   ____

3. You want to call someone near Richmond, Virginia. The local number is 528-6743. What will you dial?

____

4. You want to call someone in Helena, Montana. The local number is 721-8163. What will you dial?

____

3

A Mountain Is Full of Surprises

Preview Words/*Chapter 3*

Study the words in the box. Then read the sentences below with your teacher. Look carefully at the words in boldface type.

blown	farther	laughing	slippery
boiling	gasping	ridge	steeper
cameras	gleamed	second	surprises
crawled	higher	shoelaces	unzipped
diamonds	knocked	sideways	worth

1. Ted **unzipped** his sleeping bag and sat up.
2. The **shoelaces** were frozen stiff.
3. He **crawled** to the door of the tent.
4. The waterfall **gleamed** in the light.
5. They ran through the snow, **laughing** and shouting.
6. It was time to make camp for the **second** night.
7. At last he had a pot of **boiling** water.
8. They hiked up a long, rocky **ridge**.
9. They could see **farther** and farther away as they went up.
10. It looks like **diamonds**!
11. Well, those diamonds are **slippery**. Be careful.
12. The trail got **steeper** and steeper.
13. The wind had **blown** it away.
14. A mountain is full of **surprises**.
15. They climbed on. **Higher** and higher.
16. He saw Cathy go by him—**sideways**!
17. She was **gasping** for breath.
18. I just had the wind **knocked** out of me.
19. They hung their **cameras** under their jackets.
20. It's **worth** it!

Ted was dreaming.

The snow lay smooth and white, on and on as far as he could see. Everywhere it was smooth and white and cold. So cold.

Out there . . . There was something out there, all by itself. What was it? He couldn't see what it was. But he had to get to it. The cold ate at him, but he stumbled on through the snow.

Now he could see it. It was all by itself, sticking out of the snow. It was a ski pole . . .

Ted woke up with a start. He tried to sit up, but he couldn't move. What was going on? Where was he? "Help! Help me!" he yelled.

"What is it? What's going on?" said a voice next to him. Dennis unzipped his sleeping bag and sat up. "What is it, Ted? Are you OK?"

"Oh, Dennis, it's you! Oh . . . I was just dreaming! I'm sorry I woke you up. I just had a nightmare."

"Yes, you had a bad time of it this afternoon. But don't worry, just stay close to us and you'll be OK."

"What happened?" Emily's voice called from the other tent. "Is everyone all right over there?"

"Yes, everything is all right," Dennis called. "Go back to sleep."

"I'm sorry about this," Ted said. "I feel like a fool."

"Don't worry about it," Dennis said as he lay down and zipped up his sleeping bag. "You'd better get some sleep now. In the morning . . ." His voice faded away. He was asleep.

Ted lay awake, looking up into the dark. What a

night! He was almost afraid to go back to sleep. That nightmare—it reminded him of something. He had dreamed something like that before, hadn't he? Something about the snow . . . what was it? He tried to remember, but soon his eyes fell shut.

It seemed like a minute later when the tent shook and Cathy was calling, "Time to get up!"

"OK, OK," Dennis said. Ted could hear Cathy walking away. Dennis went back to sleep.

Ted unzipped his sleeping bag and sat up. It was still dark outside, but he could hear people moving around. Pots banged together, and someone was starting the stove.

Cold! It was cold! Ted grabbed his jacket and put it on. Then he reached around in the dark for his boots. He pulled his feet out of the sleeping bag and pushed them into the boots. *Cold!* He tried to tie his boots, but the shoelaces were frozen stiff.

Dennis turned over. "You're a real early bird!" he said sleepily.

"Cathy said that it was time to get up," Ted told him.

"I heard her," Dennis said without moving.

"And someone is making breakfast," Ted went on.

"Why didn't you say so?" Dennis unzipped his sleeping bag, sat up, and put on his jacket.

"My shoelaces are frozen," Ted said, "and I can't tie them."

"What did you think would happen?" Dennis asked as he pulled his boots out of his sleeping bag. "That's why I always sleep with my boots."

"Sleep with your boots?"

"Sure! They're warm," Dennis said, putting them on, "and I can tie my shoelaces." He crawled to the door of the tent, calling back over his shoulder, "I'm ready to go. What's keeping you?"

Ted warmed up his shoelaces with his hands, tied them as best he could, and crawled out of the tent.

It was just starting to get light, so that Ted could see the trees against the sky. The waterfall gleamed in the light from John's flashlight. "Breakfast will be ready in a minute," John called. "Get your cups ready."

When Ted got out his cup, he saw that it still had stew in it from supper. How could he clean it? He watched to see what Dennis would do.

Dennis took his cup and banged it against a tree till the bits of frozen stew fell out, then headed for the breakfast pot. Ted banged his cup against a tree a few times, then looked into it. Well, it was pretty clean, if he didn't look too closely. Was that why they ate in the dark?

Breakfast was oatmeal, lots of it. When that was all gone, they put tea into the same cups. Ted found that he didn't mind the little bits of oatmeal in his tea.

By now it was fully light. The sun would be up soon. They all hurried to pack up. The sleeping bags were stuffed into their bags, the tents were folded up, and the food was split up into the five packs. As they hit the trail, the sun lit the tops of the trees around them.

They walked through the trees for a minute or two, then suddenly they were out in the open. The sun shone brightly on the big meadow all around them, turning the snow a soft pink color.

The five people spread out so that each of them broke a new path. They ran through the deep, soft snow, laughing and shouting. Dennis fell and rolled over and over down the side of the mountain. The others laughed as he got to his feet.

"Hey, Dennis, show us that one again!"

"Not that way, Dennis! We're going *up* the mountain!"

They ran on till they got tired, and one by one they got in line again. They took turns walking at the front of the line to break the trail. Today Ted took his turn like the others.

They crossed the open meadow to the woods on the other side. But where was the trail?

They moved up and down the edge of the woods, searching. Here and there, they walked into the woods a short way. But they couldn't find anything that looked like a trail. "We'll just have to make our own trail," John said. "We can find the top of the mountain without a trail."

"I just hope the weather holds so that we can follow our own trail back down," Emily said. "If it snows, our

tracks will be all filled in, and then—"

"Oh, don't worry," Dennis cut in. "Up is up, and down is down. If we can find our way up without a trail, we can find our way down. It doesn't matter if we can't find the waterfall again. We were lucky to find it last night. Besides," he said, pointing to the sky, "just look at it! Have you ever seen a prettier day? Not a cloud in the sky! What more could you ask for? Let's go!" He headed into the woods.

All afternoon they hiked up the side of the mountain. Now, as the sun got low, they were high up on the mountain, almost to the place where no trees could grow. It was time to make camp for the second night.

"We'll be out of the wind over by these pine trees," John said.

"That's good. We'll get all the wind we need tomorrow," Emily said.

They bustled about, setting up camp. "You and Dennis are the cooks tonight," Cathy told Ted. "I'll show you what we have for supper."

Dennis got the stoves going. He took a big pot, filled it with snow, and put the pot on one of the stoves. As the snow melted down, he put more snow in, till he finally had a pot of boiling water. He threw in some rice to cook.

Ted was cooking hamburger on the other stove. "This is ready," he called.

"OK, take it off the stove. As soon as the rice is cooked, you can mix the hamburger in with it. Then I can use this stove to melt some more snow for hot chocolate," Dennis said.

As Ted mixed the hamburger into the rice, he sniffed at the steam. "This smells good! We're great cooks, aren't we! I'll have to cook this at home sometime."

Soon supper was ready. As soon as they had finished eating, they got ready for bed and got into their sleeping bags. But no one felt like sleeping. They talked and told jokes, calling from one tent to the other.

"Hey, Cathy, what's for breakfast tomorrow?"

"Oh stop it, you're as bad as Emily."

"Hey, Dennis, are you sleeping with your boots again?"

"Sure I am. Try it, you'll like it."

At last, one by one, they fell asleep.

* * * * *

Ted was dreaming again.

The snow was so white. As far as he could see, just smooth and white.

But look over there! What was it? Sticking out of the snow—it was a ski pole!

Ted woke up and stared wildly into the dark. That

nightmare again! But at least this time he knew where he was.

He lay awake for a while, turning things over in his mind. Why did he keep having the same dream? It was crazy! OK, so he had been scared when he was under the snow. But he hadn't been *that* scared, had he? And why did he dream about the ski pole? He didn't see it when he was under the snow, so why did he dream about it?

Life was funny, Ted thought. He turned over and went back to sleep.

Morning came. Ted and Dennis hurried to cook breakfast. They all ate quickly, then bustled around packing up. This was it! This was the third day, the day that they would get to the top of the mountain.

As the sky got lighter and lighter, they could see that it was a clear blue. Soon the sun would come up and warm them. Birds were hopping around in the trees over their heads. Dennis smiled from ear to ear and shouted, "What a day! I can't believe how lucky we've been! Lovely weather, day after day! This is great! When we get up to the top, we'll be able to see for miles and miles. We'll be able to see *forever.*"

"I just hope that the weather holds," Emily said. "It's a long way back down, and if it—"

"I *knew* she would say that!" Dennis said. "Didn't I tell you she would say that? Worry, worry, worry. All she ever does is worry."

Ted just laughed and put on his pack. He was all ready when Cathy yelled, "Let's get going!"

They hiked up through trees that grew small and twisted because of the wind. Soon they were where no trees could grow at all, hiking out in the open in a big, cold world of rock and ice.

They hiked up a long, rocky ridge. Outlined against the sky ahead of them, they could see piles of rocks along the ridge. The trail! The piles of rocks marked the trail to the top of the mountain. "We weren't so far off after all," John said.

As they hiked higher and higher along the ridge, they could see farther and farther away. On both sides of them, they could see mountain after mountain, mile after mile. They really did feel as if they could see forever.

Now high above them they could see the top of the mountain, with its ice-covered rocks sparkling in the sun.

"I've been here before," Ted said, "but I've never seen it look so lovely. Look how it sparkles, it looks like diamonds! It's a mountain of diamonds!"

"Well those diamonds are slippery," Emily said, "so you'd better be careful."

They ate some of their lunch, then climbed up the last ridge. The trail got steeper and steeper as they struggled up over big rocks. The wind had blown all the snow away, and everything was ice.

They stopped to take off their snowshoes and tie them to their packs. It was easier to climb without the snowshoes. But they had to be careful of deep snow in between the rocks. One time Ted stepped down and found himself up to his waist in snow. "I thought it was ice!" he said as he pulled himself out. "I thought it would hold me up!"

"A mountain is full of surprises," John told him.

They climbed on, up over rocks and ice, higher and higher.

Near the top of the mountain, the wind was blowing so hard that they had to hang onto the rocks to keep from being blown away. "Hey!" Cathy yelled suddenly. Ted looked up quickly and saw Cathy go by him—sideways! The wind was blowing her away! She flew twenty feet through the air, then bang! She hit a rock and lay still.

"Cathy!" Ted yelled as he stumbled over the rocks toward her.

"What happened?" John called.

"Is she all right?" Emily yelled.

Ted crawled over the rocks to where Cathy was lying. She lay still, her face as pale as the snow. "Cathy! Cathy! Can you hear me? Are you all right?" Ted asked.

Cathy's eyes opened and looked blindly up at the sky. She was gasping for breath. At last her face got its color back, and she seemed to see Ted for the first time. She held her hand out to him, and he slid her pack straps off her shoulders, then helped her to sit up. "I'm all right," Cathy said. "I just had the wind knocked out of me, that's all. I just couldn't get my breath."

The others came crawling over the rocks to where she sat. "Are you all right?" John asked.

"Oh, Cathy," Emily began, "you looked—"

"I'm OK now," Cathy said, standing up slowly and painfully. "Everyone take your packs off. We'll go the rest of the way to the top without them. The wind pushes on them too much. We can't risk getting blown away like that. The next person might not be so lucky. You'd better put your jackets on, too."

"Yes, Mom," Dennis said quietly. "I'm glad you're feeling like yourself again."

They took off their packs and piled them in back of a rock, after they had taken out their jackets and put them on. Emily and John took out their cameras and hung them carefully under their jackets. They all nibbled at

the food in their lunch bags. They were ready for the last climb.

At last, they were at the top! They could see off on all sides, mountain after mountain, off to the blue horizon. Mountains, roads, little towns—everything was spread out below them. "The city is over that way," John said, pointing. "We can't see it from here because it's in back of that mountain over there, the one with the flat top."

"Who wants to see the city?" Dennis asked. "This is great!"

The wind howled around them, pushing at them till they had to turn their backs to it. But they didn't mind the wind—that just made it seem more like a mountain-top. Ted held out his arms to the wind, feeling as if he could fly away like a bird. "Be careful!" Emily called. "You'll be blown away!" Ted smiled at her, but he put his arms down.

They were starting to get cold. Quickly John and

Emily got out their cameras and took some pictures of the others standing in front of the mountains spread out below them. "This will show those city people what they missed!" Dennis said.

They turned and climbed back down the way they had come till they got back to their packs. "One thing gets to me about winter hiking," Dennis said as he put his pack on.

"What's that?" Ted asked.

"You spend three days getting up to the top of a mountain. Then when you get there you can stay only fifteen or twenty minutes before you get so cold that you have to go back down again."

"Yes, but it's worth it. It's really something up there! You feel so strong and free!" Ted said. "And it's so pretty! You will always have the picture in your mind."

"So you're glad you came?" Dennis asked.

"I sure am! Winter hiking is great!" Ted told him. "Who cares about frozen shoelaces? Who cares about nightmares? It's all worth it. And getting down again will be the easy part."

John looked over at him. "A mountain is full of surprises," he said.

Comprehension Questions*/Chapter 3*

Directions. Answer these questions about the chapter you have just read. Put an *x* in the box beside the best answer to each question.

1. (D) How did the others feel when Ted yelled in his sleep?

   - ☐ a. They thought he was silly for being such a fool.
   - ☐ b. They wished that he had not come on the trip.
   - ☐ c. They were mad because he woke them up.
   - ☒ d. They were afraid that something bad had happened to him.

2. (B) Why couldn't Ted tie his shoelaces in the morning?

   - ☐ a. He couldn't bend the shoelaces because they were frozen.
   - ☐ b. He couldn't bend the shoelaces because his hands hurt.
   - ☐ c. Someone had taken the shoelaces out of his boots.
   - ☐ d. Someone had cut his shoelaces.

3. (A) Dennis said, "I'm ready to go. *What's keeping you?*" What is another way of saying this?

- ☐ a. Who is taking care of you?
- ☐ b. Why are you so slow?
- ☐ c. Where did you put your things?
- ☐ d. What are you holding onto?

4. (A) Dennis said, "When we get to the top of the mountain, *we'll be able to see forever!*" What did he mean?

- ☐ a. They would always stay on the top of the mountain.
- ☐ b. They would see into the future.
- ☐ c. They would see things that were many miles away.
- ☐ d. They would see nothing but the sky.

5. (B) Why did Cathy fall?

- ☐ a. She stumbled over a rock.
- ☐ b. The wind picked her up and blew her.
- ☐ c. She fell over Ted's pack.
- ☐ d. She stepped on her own snowshoe.

6. (C) Which of these things happened last?

- ☐ a. Ted ran to help Cathy.
- ☐ b. Cathy flew through the air.
- ☐ c. Cathy told everyone to take off their packs.
- ☐ d. Cathy looked as pale as the snow.

7. (C) Which of these things happened last?

- ☐ a. They got to the top of the mountain.
- ☐ b. Cathy fell.
- ☐ c. Ted and Dennis cooked supper.
- ☐ d. They climbed up across the meadow.

8. (D) Why were there no trees on the top of the mountain?

- ☐ a. Someone had cut them all down.
- ☐ b. Trees could not grow because there was no water.
- ☐ c. Trees could not grow because the wind was so strong.
- ☐ d. The snow had bent down all the trees.

9. (E) Why did they climb to the top of the mountain?

- ☐ a. It was part of their work.
- ☐ b. They had to go back for something they had left there on another trip.
- ☐ c. They liked being on the top because it made them feel strong and free.
- ☐ d. They liked being on the top because the wind was not very strong there.

10. (E) What did John mean when he said, "A mountain is full of surprises"?

- ☐ a. Mountains offer many wonderful sights.
- ☐ b. They never knew what might happen next.
- ☐ c. They knew that the weather would be lovely.
- ☐ d. They kept finding new people on the mountain.

Skills Used to Answer Questions

A. Recognizing Words in Context
B. Recalling Facts
C. Keeping Events in Order
D. Making Inferences
E. Understanding Main Ideas

Using Prefixes to Make New Words

You know that a prefix is a group of letters added to the beginning of a word to change its meaning. You have learned how to use prefixes to figure out new words.

Here is a review of the prefixes you have learned:

Prefix	Meaning	Example
un- →	not →	unhappy
re- →	again →	rewrite
anti- →	against →	antirust
pre- →	before →	preheat
mis- →	wrong →	misread
inter- →	between →	interstate
non- →	not →	nonstop
sub- →	under, below →	submarine
semi- →	half →	semiprivate
dis- →	not →	dishonest

When you know how to add prefixes to words, you can make many new words. For example, suppose you want to say *make again.* You know that the prefix *re-* means *again.* You can add *re-* to *make* to get the new word *remake. Remake* means *make again.* How would you say *cook again?*

____

Exercise 1

Practice making new words by adding prefixes. Below are some words without prefixes. Add a prefix to each word to give it the meaning that is asked for.

To make a new word, follow these steps:

1. Look at the review box of prefixes and meanings at the beginning of this lesson.
2. Find the prefix that has the meaning you want.
3. Add the prefix to the old word. Print the new word on the line.

The first one has been done for you.

1. **plant** (Make a word that means *plant again.*)

   replant
   ___

2. **mixed** (Make a word that means *mixed before.*)

   ___

3. **surface** (Make a word that means *below the surface.*)

   ___

4. **pave** (Make a word that means *pave again.*)

   ___

5. **theft** (Make a word that means *against theft.*)

   ___

6. **read** (Make a word that means *read wrong.*)

   ___

7. **weave** (Make a word that means *weave between.*)

____

Exercise 2

Each sentence below has a word missing. Complete each sentence by making a word with a prefix and printing it in the blank space. The words in dark print after the sentence will tell you the meaning of the word you should make. To find the prefix you need, look back at the review box of prefixes and meanings at the beginning of the lesson. For help in making a new word, use the steps given in Exercise 1. The first one has been done for you.

1. Jane misspelled three words on her homework. **(spelled wrong)**

2. I like this story so much that I want to ____________ it. **(read again)**

3. The whole class laughed when Phil ____________ Leroy's last name. **(pronounced wrong)**

4. Tony gave his car a coat of ____________ paint. **(against rust)**

5. Baseball teams play their ____________ games in the South. **(before the season)**

6. In Maine, winter temperatures are often ____________. **(below zero)**

7. The insurance paid for a ____________ room in the hospital. **(half private)**

Directory Assistance

You know how to find a local phone number in the phone book. You also know how to find area codes for long distance calls. But sometimes you will need help to get the phone number you want. Then you can call *Directory Assistance.* That means that you call a special phone number and an operator will try to find the number you need.

Local Calls

Most local numbers are listed in the phone book. But sometimes you might not be able to find the number you need. If you cannot find a local phone number, you can call Directory Assistance. The number for local Directory Assistance is 411.

Long Distance Calls

Your local phone book lists only local numbers. To get the number of someone who lives outside your area, you must call long distance Directory Assistance.

To get long distance Directory Assistance, you must dial 1, the area code of the area you want to call, and 555-1212. A list of long distance area codes is given at the front of the phone book.

> To call long distance Directory Assistance, follow these steps:
>
> 1. Find the area code of the place you want to call.
> 2. Dial *1 + the area code + 555-1212.*

When you call either local or long distance Directory Assistance, the operator will ask you two questions:

1. What *city* do you want to call?
2. What is the *name* of the person or business you want to call?

You must tell the operator the place you want to call. Then you must tell the operator the full name of the person you want to call. You should also tell the operator the person's address. If there are several people with the same name in the place you are calling, the operator may not be able to give you the right number without an address.

Suppose you want to call Margaret Hill of Richmond, Virginia. You do not know her phone number. You know that her address is 54 Oak Street.

You look at the area code list in your phone book. The area code for Richmond, Virginia is 804. You call Directory Assistance to get Margaret Hill's phone number.

1. Print the number you will dial to call Directory Assistance.

   ____

2. The operator says, "What city, please?" Print your answer.

   ____

3. The operator says, "What is the name, please?" Print your answer.

   ____

Charges for Directory Assistance

If you call Directory Assistance to get a local number, you may be charged for your call. So before using Directory Assistance, always look in your phone book for the number you want. Use Directory Assistance only if you cannot find the number in the book.

Calling Directory Assistance

You know that you can dial *411* to get a local number from Directory Assistance. You call *1 + the area code + 555-1212* to get a long distance number from Directory Assistance. You also know that long distance area codes are listed in your phone book. Here is a list of area codes:

LONG DISTANCE CALLING

area codes for some cities

place	area code
DISTRICT OF COLUMBIA	
Washington, D.C.	202
FLORIDA	
Jacksonville	904
Miami	305
St. Petersburg	813
Tampa	813
GEORGIA	
Atlanta	404
Augusta	404
Columbus	404
Savannah	912
HAWAII	
All Points	808
IDAHO	
All Points	208
ILLINOIS	
Chicago	312
Decatur	217
East St. Louis	618
Evanston	312
Joliet	815
Peoria	309
Rockford	815
Springfield	217
MONTANA	
All Points	406
NEBRASKA	
Grand Island	308
Lincoln	402
Omaha	402
NEVADA	
All Points	702
NEW HAMPSHIRE	
All Points	603
NEW JERSEY	
Atlantic City	609
Bayonne	201
Camden	609
Clifton	201
Elizabeth	201
Jersey City	201
Newark	201
Orange	201
Paterson	201
Trenton	609
Woodbridge	201
NEW MEXICO	
All Points	505
OKLAHOMA	
Oklahoma City	405
Tulsa	918
OREGON	
All Points	503
PENNSYLVANIA	
Allentown	215
Altonna	814
Bethlehem	215
Chester	215
Easton	215
Erie	814
Harrisburg	717
Haverford	215
Johnstown	814
Lancaster	717
Philadelphia	215
Pittsburgh	412
Reading	215
Scranton	717
Wilkes-Barre	717
RHODE ISLAND	
All Points	401
SOUTH CAROLINA	
All Points	803

Exercise 1

Look at the cases below. For each one, what number would you dial to get Directory Assistance? Print your answers on the lines. The first two have been done for you.

> Follow these steps:
> 1. Decide if the call is local or long distance.
> 2. If the call is local, you should dial local Directory Assistance, *411.*
> 3. If the call is long distance, you should first find the area code on the list above. Then you should dial *1 + the area code + 555-1212.*

1. You live in Illinois. You want to get the number of a friend who just moved to your town.

   411
   ____

2. You live in New York. You want to get the number of a business in Omaha, Nebraska.

   1 + 402 + 555 - 1212
   ____

3. You live in Florida. You want to get the number of a new restaurant near your house.

   ____

4. You live in Pennsylvania. You want to get the number of a friend in Montana.

   ____

5. You live in Nevada. You want to get the number of a store in Newark, New Jersey.

____

Exercise 2

You know that to get a number from Directory Assistance you must tell the operator the place and the person you want to call. You should also give the operator the person's address if you know it.

Look at each of the following calls to Directory Assistance. On the lines provided, print your answers to the operator's questions. The first one has been done for you.

1. You want the number of John P. Greene of 15 Ivy Street, Dallas, Texas.

   What city please? Dallas

   What name please? John P. Greene, 15 Ivy Street

2. You want the number of Maria Garcia of 98 Lookout Drive, Ithaca, N.Y.

   What city please? _______________

   What name please? _______________

3. You want the number of the Shady Top Motel in Harrisburg, Pennsylvania.

   What city please? _______________

   What name please? _______________

4. You want the number of the Sears-Roebuck store in Sacramento, California.

What city please? ______________________

What name please? ______________________

4

The Nightmare Begins

Preview Words/*Chapter 4*

Study the words in the box. Then read the sentences below with your teacher. Look carefully at the words in boldface type.

aid	fourth	matches	shock
broken	gear	moment	storm
chances	hood	rattled	strongest
fingers	keys	rescue	tighter
flap	leave	screamed	valley

1. Morning came on the **fourth** day.
2. Now, tie this **tighter** over here.
3. For a **moment**, he looked down at them.
4. "Dennis!" Emily **screamed**.
5. He's going to go into **shock** out here.
6. His right leg looks **broken**.
7. She zipped up the sleeping bag and pulled the **hood** up around his head.
8. You and John are the **strongest** hikers.
9. He grabbed some **matches**.
10. He put a first **aid** kit in his pack.
11. It will take some time to get a **rescue** team.
12. Cathy gave Emily her car **keys**.
13. Be careful. Don't take any **chances**.
14. Big, dark clouds were rolling up from the **valley**.
15. Ted could see that a big **storm** was coming.
16. They put the **gear** into the tent.
17. The snow **rattled** against the tent.
18. Ted shone a flashlight out through the **flap** of the tent.
19. We won't **leave** you.
20. His hand was so cold that he could hardly bend his **fingers**.

They hiked back down along the ridge the way they had come, following the piles of rocks that marked the trail. When they got back down to the trees, they followed their own path. Because the snow was all packed down, they could go very fast.

They camped in the same place they had the night before. No one talked much. They ate and then went right to bed. They went to sleep quickly.

* * * * *

Ted was dreaming.

He was stumbling through the snow. He had to find something. But what was it? What did he have to find? Something . . .

A ski pole! That was it! He had to find the ski pole! Somewhere in the snow . . .

The wind was blowing hard. The snow blew around him—blew into his eyes so that he couldn't see. But still he stumbled on through the deep snow. The ski pole—he had to find the ski pole.

Ted woke up and looked around him in the dark tent. That nightmare again! Why did he keep dreaming it over and over? Oh well, he wasn't going to think about it in the middle of the night. He turned over and went back to sleep.

Morning came on the fourth day. When they got up, it was already getting light. But they didn't have to hurry any more—they were on their way down.

As it got lighter, they could see that the sky was not clear. There were thin, high clouds covering the sky. "Oh no," Emily said. "Look! There's bad weather coming in!"

"Oh come on, Emily," Dennis said, "it's just a little cloudy, that's all. It's not going to storm today."

"Well, I just wouldn't want to be out in that meadow in a storm."

"We won't be! We'll get through that today, and then we're almost home. There isn't a thing to worry about."

"Come on, you two!" Cathy called. "Stop talking and get your things packed. It's time to hit the trail."

"What's your hurry?" Dennis asked. But he headed for the tent.

The hike down the mountain went quickly. Where it was steep, they could ski down on their snowshoes, squatting and sliding on the smooth, packed snow. It was great fun. Ted felt as if he were flying.

But the rest of the trip down was not as easy as he had thought it would be. It was hard to walk down a hill on snowshoes, almost harder than going up. His foot kept slipping through the open part of the snowshoe and getting stuck. Every time it happened, he would have to sit down, take off the snowshoe, and put it on again. And getting up again with the pack on wasn't easy!

"It happens to the best of us," John said as he walked by where Ted was sitting.

"Look, Ted," Cathy said as she came over to him, "tie your snowshoe tighter on this side to keep it from slipping. And don't sit in the snow like that or you'll get wet. Now tie this tighter over here, like this. Now let me show you—when you come to a steep place, step down *this* way. Not that way, *this* way."

"OK, OK," Ted said. He walked away from Cathy as quickly as he could. He was almost mad when his snowshoes didn't get stuck again.

They walked down across the open meadow. They could go so fast on a packed trail! Before they knew it, they were back to the waterfall. "It isn't really time to make camp yet," John said. "Does anyone want to go on?"

"Maybe we should," Emily said. "I still don't like the look of those clouds."

"But then we'd get home a day early!" Dennis said. "And this will be the last trip this winter. Let's stay! We can look around and just have fun in the woods, and then we can have a big supper. What do you say? Let's stay!"

"I *would* like to take some more pictures," John said.

"I don't need to get home till tomorrow," Cathy said.

"I'm happy here," Ted said.

"Oh all right," Emily said. "But don't say I didn't tell you."

They took off their packs and put them in a pile. John went off with his camera. "Who wants to see where the waterfall comes from?" Dennis asked.

"I'll go with you," Cathy said. "Let's go up over here." They took off their snowshoes and began to climb along the side of the waterfall.

Ted and Emily opened their packs and dug out their lunch bags and their jackets. Then they sat on their packs to eat and talk. After a while, John came back and sat with them. "It sure is peaceful," Ted said. "It feels as if nothing bad could ever happen here."

Just then they heard Dennis's voice calling, "Hey! Up here!"

They looked up. Dennis was standing at the very top of the waterfall, twenty feet above them, waving. They could see Cathy climbing slowly down the side of the waterfall. "It's really great up here!" Dennis called. "You should come up! Just think of it—I'm standing on a waterfall! Doesn't that sound funny?"

"Dennis! Be careful!" Emily shouted. "That's ice—

it's slippery! You might fall!"

"Oh, stop worrying," Dennis said. "You take all the fun out of life."

Now Cathy had climbed down. She walked over to where the others were standing and yelled, "Dennis, get down here! You have no right to fool around like that! If you fall . . ."

"Oh all right! I'm coming!" Dennis said. He turned to walk back into the woods. But as he turned, his foot slipped. He turned sideways out into the air above them. For a moment, he looked down at them, his mouth open in a shout that he never had time to give.

Then he fell.

Below him, the others stood frozen, watching him fall. They watched him hit the ice. They saw his hands grab for a hold, then slip. They watched him slide over the ice and fall into the snow below. "Dennis!" Emily screamed. Her voice hung in the quiet woods.

They ran, stumbling in the deep snow, struggling to push their way through it. Ted felt as if he were swimming in deep water. But John still had his snowshoes on, so he reached Dennis first.

"Dennis! Dennis! Oh, God! Dennis!" John was crying. He had taken off one snowshoe and was digging the snow away from Dennis as the others stumbled up.

Ted threw himself down beside Dennis. "He's breathing! He's still alive!"

"Oh, what are we going to do?" Cathy cried.

"The first thing to do is to keep him warm," Emily said. "Come on! We don't have time to cry. I don't think he hit his head on the way down. But he's going to go into shock out here."

"You're right," said John. He jumped up, put his

snowshoe back on, and ran to the packs. He pulled out his sleeping bag and pad and ran back to where Dennis was lying.

They spread out the pad next to Dennis. Then they unzipped the sleeping bag all the way and spread it open on the pad. Carefully, they moved Dennis into the bag. "His right leg looks broken," said John.

"I think you're right. But we have to get him warm first," said Emily. She zipped up the sleeping bag and pulled the hood up around his head.

"Now what do we do?" Ted asked. "Oh, if only he would wake up."

"We can't wait for that," John said. "He needs help, and he needs it fast. We're going to have to get him out of here."

"We can't move him," Emily said. "We have to keep him quiet. Some of us will have to go for help."

"Emily, you and John are the strongest hikers," Cathy said. "You go. I'll stay here and take care of Dennis and Ted. I mean—and Ted will help me."

"OK." Emily put on her snowshoes while John grabbed his pack and took everything out. He grabbed some matches and a first aid kit and put them back into the pack. Emily pushed in her sleeping bag, and they packed their jackets in on top.

"It will be dark soon," John said. "We have a good, packed trail, so we'll get down all right. But we may have to drive quite a way to get help, and it will take some time to get a rescue team. We may not be back much before morning."

Cathy gave Emily her car keys. "Be careful," she said. "Don't take any chances."

"We'll be back as soon as we can," Emily said. And then they were gone.

Cathy and Ted turned back to Dennis. He was very pale, and his breath was going in and out in short gasps. "He's in shock," Cathy said. "If they don't get back in time he'll die."

Ted unzipped the sleeping bag part way to feel Dennis's hands. "He's cold," Ted said. "How about another sleeping bag?"

"OK," Cathy said. She got Dennis's sleeping bag out of his pack. They put Dennis into the sleeping bag and zipped it over the other bag, then put Emily's pack under his feet.

"Let's set up camp," Cathy said. "The tent will help

keep him warm. And we need to eat. We have to stay strong."

They got Ted's tent and laid it out next to Dennis. As they put it up, Ted kept looking over at Dennis, so pale and strange. Ted looked around at the woods. They seemed white and strange too.

Ted was glad that he wasn't alone with Dennis. Cathy's voice sounded good to him, even when she was telling him how to put up his own tent.

Carefully, slowly, they pulled the pad with Dennis on it into the tent. Then Ted got a stove going while Cathy got out the food. Cathy started melting a pot of snow. "I'm going out to the meadow to have a look around," Ted said.

"Don't go too far," Cathy said. "I can't leave Dennis alone to go look for you."

"I'll be all right," Ted said. He put on his snowshoes and walked up the path they had made. He walked out into the open and looked up at the sky. He gasped.

The sky was black. Big, dark clouds were rolling up from the valley. Already they hid the woods on the other side of the meadow. In the last light of the day, Ted could see that a big storm was coming. Soon.

It was getting dark fast as Ted hurried back to the camp. "There's a storm coming!" he told Cathy. "It's rolling in fast!"

"Oh no! Really? Well, John and Emily should be almost to the car by now, if they haven't had any bad luck. They'll get out all right. But they won't get back in. The rescue team won't get to us till the storm stops. Maybe it will blow over quickly." She looked back at the tent where Dennis was lying. "It has to," she said quietly.

They ate quickly, then put all the gear into the tent,

even the snowshoes and ski poles. Then they crawled in and sat down to wait.

The wind started to blow, quietly at first, then harder and harder. Even the pine trees around them couldn't protect them from the wind. The tent shook and jumped as the wind hit it.

Then it started to snow.

The snow rattled against the tent and piled up along the sides. It blew over and around them. Ted shone a flashlight out through the flap of the tent, but all he could see was a moving wall of white.

Dennis lay pale and still. His breathing was better, but he never moved.

Suddenly he began to moan, "Oh . . . Oh . . ."

Cathy bent over him and asked, "What is it, Dennis? What's the matter? Can I do anything for you?"

Suddenly Dennis started to shout, "I'm coming! Wait for me! I'm coming!" His eyes flew open and he looked around blindly. He tried to sit up. "Wait for me! I'm coming!"

"Oh my God, he's out of his head!" Cathy said. "Ted! Quick! Help me hold him down!"

Ted quickly crawled over, put his hands on Dennis's arms, and pushed him back down. "It's OK, Dennis," he said. "It's OK, old friend. We'll wait for you. We'll wait."

Dennis lay back, quiet. "Don't leave me," he said again. "Don't leave me. Wait for me."

"We won't leave you," Cathy told him. "We're right here."

"We won't leave you," Ted went on, patting Dennis's arm. "We'll wait."

Outside the wind howled around the tent. The tent shook as if a big hand were hitting it. The snow rattled over them.

The tent shook harder and harder, till the sides were

flapping up and down. Suddenly the tent fell in on them. They were hit by the cold, flapping cloth. "The tent is down!" Cathy shouted.

"I can see that!" Ted said. "I'll go out and see what I can do."

"Don't go away from the tent, or you'll get lost!" Cathy told him.

"I'll be careful," Ted said as he crawled out under the flapping cloth. When he got outside, the wind hit at him so hard that he could hardly stand. The snow blew into his face, into his eyes, *just like in his nightmares.*

He grabbed for the top of the tent and pulled it up till the tent was standing again. Suddenly it flapped and pulled against him so that he almost fell down on top of it. He pulled it up again and found the rope which was still tied to the tent. Now where was the tree that it had been tied to?

Holding the rope, he began to walk away from the tent. He could hardly move against the wind. He took one step and fell into the soft snow. He got up and took another step, and another. Suddenly he banged into something hard. The tree! He pulled on the rope and tried to get it around the tree. When the wind dropped for a moment, he quickly pulled the rope around.

Ted stood hanging onto the rope, leaning against the wind, thinking about what to do next. How could he tie the rope with his big mittens on? He took off one mitten and put it under the other arm. Right away, his hand became so cold that he could hardly bend his fingers. He had to! He tied the rope as well as he could, knotting it over and over. "I sure hope this holds," he said. "I don't want to have to do this again."

Suddenly the wind picked up again. His mitten flew away from him and flapped against the end of its strap till Ted grabbed it and put it on. Thank God for that

strap! He had laughed at it when he got the mittens at the camping store five days ago. But what would he do without it now?

The camping store! Had he ever been in that store? Or had he always been on this mountain, fighting the wind? He turned to go back to the tent.

Where *was* the tent?

He was four steps away from it, but which way? He couldn't see it at all. "Cathy!" he shouted. "Cathy, where are you?" But all he could hear was the howling of the wind.

The rope! He reached up, feeling around in the blinding snow for the rope. At last his arm bumped against it. He grabbed it with both hands and followed it. One step. Two steps. Three. Four. Where was the tent? At last his hand bumped into the flapping cloth.

He crawled in through the tent flap. "Where have you

been?" Cathy asked. "I was getting worried. You look like a snowman."

Ted looked down at himself. He was all white from head to foot. He brushed himself off as well as he could and pulled off his jacket. He was so tired. In all his life he had never been so tired. He crawled over to his sleeping bag and got into it, boots and all. "You watch over Dennis for a while," he told Cathy. "Wake me up if the tent starts to fall down again. I've got to get some sleep."

He didn't care if he had that nightmare again, he thought as he zipped up his sleeping bag. The nightmare could never be as bad as what was really outside the tent.

A moment later he was asleep.

Comprehension Questions/*Chapter 4*

Directions. Answer these questions about the chapter you have just read. Put an *x* in the box beside the best answer to each question.

1. (E) What is the main thing that happened in this part of the story?

☐ a. Dennis was hurt.
☐ b. The tent fell down.
☐ c. John and Emily went back to the car.
☐ d. Ted put the tent back up.

2. (B) Why were they able to come down the mountain much faster than they went up?

☐ a. They took a shortcut.
☐ b. The snow on the trail was packed down.
☐ c. They ran most of the way.
☐ d. The snow had been blown away by the wind.

3. (D) How did Cathy feel about Ted?

☐ a. She thought he was a very good hiker.
☐ b. She thought that he couldn't take care of himself.
☐ c. She didn't like him at all.
☐ d. She thought that he was being mean to Emily.

4. (A) Emily said, "There's *bad weather coming in!*" What does that mean?

☐ a. The snow was blowing into the tent.
☐ b. It looked as if Cathy and Ted were going to argue.
☐ c. She felt bad because it was snowing.
☐ d. She could see that there would soon be a storm.

5. (C) Which of these things happened first?

☐ a. Dennis and Cathy climbed up the waterfall.
☐ b. Dennis called down to the others.
☐ c. Dennis fell.
☐ d. Emily yelled, "Be careful!"

6. (A) "It isn't really time to make camp yet," John said. "Does anyone want to *go on?*" What does that mean?

☐ a. Does anyone want to climb the waterfall?
☐ b. Does anyone want to go to the camping spot?
☐ c. Does anyone want to keep walking down the mountain?
☐ d. Does anyone want to walk faster?

7. (D) Why did John take almost everything out of his pack when he was going for help?

- ☐ a. He thought that Dennis needed the things.
- ☐ b. He wanted to make his pack light so that he could hike faster.
- ☐ c. He was looking for something in his pack.
- ☐ d. He wanted to make more room in his pack for Dennis's things.

8. (C) Which of these things happened last?

- ☐ a. The tent fell down.
- ☐ b. Ted lost his mitten.
- ☐ c. Ted got into his sleeping bag.
- ☐ d. Ted brushed himself off.

9. (B) How did Ted get back to the tent after he had tied it up again?

- ☐ a. He called to Cathy to come and get him.
- ☐ b. He followed the rope.
- ☐ c. He crawled back over the ice.
- ☐ d. He waited till morning.

10. (E) This chapter of the story is called "The Nightmare Begins." Why is that a good title?

- ☐ a. Ted had a nightmare for the first time.
- ☐ b. The events in Ted's nightmare began to come true.
- ☐ c. All the others began to have nightmares.
- ☐ d. Ted was afraid of snow because of his nightmare.

Skills Used to Answer Questions

A. Recognizing Words in Context
B. Recalling Facts
C. Keeping Events in Order
D. Making Inferences
E. Understanding Main Ideas

Suffixes

A suffix is a group of letters added to the end of a word. A suffix changes the meaning of a word. For example, the suffix *-ful* means *full of.* You know that *delight* means *pleasure.* If you add *-ful* to the end of *delight,* you make the word *delightful. Delightful* means *full of pleasure* or *full of delight.*

The suffix *-ly* means *done in a certain way.* The word *quick* means *fast.* If you add the suffix *-ly* to the word *quick,* you get *quickly. Quickly* means *done in a quick way* or *done fast.*

The suffix *-less* means *without.* If you add *-less* to the word *color,* you get the new word *colorless. Colorless* means *without color.*

Here are some common suffixes and their meanings:

Suffix	Meaning	Example
-en →	to make →	lighten
-ly →	done in a certain way →	quickly
-ful →	full of →	delightful
-less →	without →	colorless
-ness →	a state of being →	greatness
-able →	able to be →	changeable

Exercise 1

Each word below has a suffix. Underline the suffix in each word. Then print it in the space below the word. The first one has been done for you.

1. lengthen

   en

2. nicely

   ______

3. thoughtless

   ______

4. wonderful

   ______

5. washable

   ______

6. sadness

   ______

Exercise 2

Each sentence below has a word with a suffix. Find the word with the suffix and print it on the line. Then draw a circle around the suffix in the word. The first one has been done for you.

1. You may catch cold if you go out hatless in the winter.

   hatless

2. This old coat is not wearable.

   ______

3. José uses sugar to sweeten his tea.

   ______

4. She was well-known for her goodness.

____

5. Kevin had a painful toothache.

____

6. Angela ran the race smoothly.

____

Exercise 3

In this exercise, each word on the left has a suffix. The list on the right gives the meanings of words. Find the meaning on the right that goes best with each word on the left. Use the box that shows suffixes and their meanings at the beginning of the chapter to help you. Print the meaning on the line next to the word. The first one has been done for you.

1. dampen to make damp	state of being weak
2. mildness __________	able to be returned
3. returnable __________	without harm
4. dampness __________	to make weak
5. harmless __________	to make damp
6. weakness __________	done in a mild way
7. inhabitable __________	state of being damp

8. harmful ____________________ state of being mild

9. weaken ____________________ able to be inhabited

10. mildly ____________________ full of harm

Rates for Long Distance Calls: Part One

You know that when you make a local call you dial only the seven-digit local phone number. When you make a long distance phone call, you dial *1 + the area code + the phone number.*

You must pay extra for long distance calls. The charges for long distance calls are called *rates.* The cost of a long distance call is not always the same. Long distance rates are based on the distance to the place you are calling, and on the amount of time you talk. They also depend on the time of day and the day of the week.

Calls made during the day cost more than calls made at night. Calls made during the week cost more than calls made on weekends. The *rate periods* are given at the beginning of your phone book. By looking at the rate period table, you can figure out when it would be cheapest to make your call.

Here is a sample table of rate periods from the phone book:

long distance calls rate periods		
	MON-FRI	SAT & SUN
8 AM to 5 PM	DAY Full Rate	
5 PM to 11 PM	EVENING Approximately 35% Lower Than Day Rate	
11 PM to 8 AM	NIGHT AND WEEKEND Approximately 60% Lower Than Day Rate	

HOLIDAYS
January 1, July 4, Labor Day, Thanksgiving Day, December 25. The Evening rate applies all day.

This table shows four different rate periods:

1. **Day.** You pay the *day rate* if you make a call between 8:00 A.M. and 5:00 P.M. on Monday through Friday.
2. **Evening.** You pay the *evening rate* if you make a call after 5:00 P.M. and before 11:00 P.M. on Monday through Friday. The evening rate is cheaper than the day rate.
3. **Night and Weekend.** You pay the *night rate* if you make a call after 11:00 P.M. and before 8:00 A.M. on Monday through Friday. You pay the *weekend rate* if you make a call any time on Saturday, and Sunday until 5:00 P.M. Night and weekend rates are the same. They are the cheapest.
4. **Holidays.** You pay the *evening rate* if you make a call between 8:00 A.M. and 5:00 P.M. on certain holidays.

Suppose you want to call someone at 10:00 on a weekday morning. You will pay the *day rate* for your call. You will pay the *evening rate* if you call at 10:00 at night. You will pay the *night rate* if you call at 11:30 at night.

Use the table to answer the questions below. Circle your answers.

1. What rate will you pay if you make a long distance call at 3:00 on Wednesday afternoon?

   Day Rate   Evening Rate   Night and Weekend Rate

2. What rate will you pay if you make a call at 8:00 on Saturday night?

Day Rate	Evening Rate	Night and Weekend Rate

3. What rate will you pay if you make a call at 7:30 on Friday morning?

Day Rate	Evening Rate	Night and Weekend Rate

4. What rate will you pay if you make a call at 9:15 A.M. on Christmas?

Day Rate	Evening Rate	Night and Weekend Rate

In-State and Out-of-State Calls

Your local phone company handles long-distance calls within your home state. The daytime, evening, night and weekend rates are charged for in-state long distance calls.

There are several different out-of-state long distance phone companies. You can choose any company you want as your out-of-state company. Each company charges different rates. Many out-of-state long distance companies charge lower rates for evening, night and weekend calls. Some do not. Ask your company for a rate table. The table will tell you the company's rates for out-of-state long distance calls.

Rates for Long Distance Calls: Part One

You know that rates for long distance calls are highest during the day from Monday through Friday. Calls made at night and on weekends cost less. Also, the longer you talk, the more your call will cost.

The rate table in your phone book looks like this:

<table>
<tr><th colspan="3">long distance calls
rate periods</th></tr>
<tr><th></th><th>MON-FRI</th><th>SAT & SUN</th></tr>
<tr><td>8 AM
to
5 PM</td><td>DAY
Full Rate</td><td rowspan="3">NIGHT AND WEEKEND
Approximately 60% Lower
Than Day Rate</td></tr>
<tr><td>5 PM
to
11 PM</td><td>EVENING
Approximately 35% Lower
Than Day Rate</td></tr>
<tr><td>11 PM
to
8 AM</td><td>NIGHT AND WEEKEND
Approximately 60% Lower
Than Day Rate</td></tr>
</table>

HOLIDAYS
January 1, July 4, Labor Day, Thanksgiving Day, December 25. The Evening rate applies all day.

The table tells you the rates for different times of day and different days of the week.

Exercise

Look at the times of the day and the days of the week given in the exercise below. If you make a long distance phone call at each of these times, what rate will you pay? Use the rate table to find out if you must pay the *day rate,* the *evening rate* or the *night and weekend rate.*

Follow these steps:

1. Look at the top of the table for the day of the week.
2. Look at the left side of the chart for the time of day.
3. See what box your call falls in. Is it *Day, Evening* or *Night & Weekend?*

Print your answers in the spaces provided. The first one has been done for you.

1. 8:00 Monday evening evening rate
2. 6:45 Thursday morning __________
3. 4:00 Tuesday afternoon __________
4. 2:30 Saturday afternoon __________
5. 11:30 Wednesday morning __________
6. 8:30 Sunday evening __________
7. 10:00 A.M. on Labor Day __________
8. 11:45 P.M. on Wednesday __________

5

The Ski Pole

Study the words in the box. Then read the sentences below with your teacher. Look carefully at the words in boldface type.

check	least	slept	uphill
choke	passed	spoonful	weaker
daytime	plane	strength	whenever
downhill	scarf	tasted	word
foolish	shape	trace	yesterday

1. In his nightmare, it had been **daytime**.
2. He could see a **shape** in the dark.
3. Time **passed** slowly.
4. Ted **slept** for a while.
5. At **least** his mouth was full for a moment.
6. He tied his **scarf** around his neck.
7. I'm going to **check** the ropes.
8. Without saying a **word**, she handed him some chocolate.
9. He had never **tasted** anything so good in his life.
10. He hasn't had anything to eat since **yesterday**.
11. That will make him even **weaker**.
12. Wouldn't the food make him **choke**?
13. He's got to keep his **strength** up.
14. Dennis ate the **spoonful** of oatmeal.
15. **Whenever** Dennis moved, they fed him.
16. At last there would be no **trace** of her.
17. The trail went out into the meadow, then **uphill**.
18. Then it turned and went **downhill**.
19. I thought I heard a **plane**.
20. We can't do **foolish** things.

Ted was dreaming.

The wind was howling. The snow beat against him, stinging his face and getting into his eyes. He couldn't see where he was going. But he had to keep going. He had to keep on. He had to look for someone. He had to find her.

When he woke up, it seemed as if he were still asleep. The wind was still howling, and the snow beat against the tent. But it was dark. In his nightmare it had been daytime.

He turned his head. He could see a shape in the dark. It was Cathy sitting up in her sleeping bag. "How is Dennis?" Ted asked. "Is he any better?"

"I don't know. I can't see him. He didn't wake up at all, but his breathing is OK, and he has been quiet."

"Well that's good, I think. If you want to get some sleep now, I'll stay awake and watch him."

"OK," Cathy said as she lay down. "Wake me up if you need me."

"Right."

Ted lay there in the dark. It felt funny to have his boots on in his sleeping bag. At last he got out of his sleeping bag and took them off. The shoelaces were not frozen. "You were right, Dennis," Ted said softly, "you *should* put your boots in your sleeping bag." He put the boots back in the sleeping bag, then got in and lay down.

The wind howled around the tent. When the wind dropped for a moment, Ted could hear Dennis breathing. Everything seemed to be OK for the moment.

But what were they going to do next?

Where were John and Emily? Had they made it back to the car before the storm hit? Or were they out there somewhere, lost in the storm? They wouldn't even have a tent to hide them from the wind and snow.

If they did get to the car, what would they do? A rescue team could not go out in this storm. They would have to wait till the storm was over.

Then what? All their tracks would be gone. Would the rescue team ever find them? It was good that they had camped by the waterfall. Sooner or later the rescue team would find the waterfall. But would it be too late for Dennis?

Ted just lay there and looked into the dark. Time passed slowly. What time *was* it? Would morning ever come? Ted tried to think about something nice. A good hot breakfast—that would be nice right now. Ted thought about what he would like to eat for breakfast. He would start with—

"No! No! Don't do that!" Dennis was shouting. Ted could feel him rolling around on the pad. "No! No! Stop!"

"Dennis! It's all right! I'm here!" Ted said. He tried to grab Dennis, but Dennis broke away from him. He seemed so strong!

Cathy sat up and said, "Ted! What are we going to do?"

"Help me hold him down! He's going to hurt himself! We can't let him roll around like this!" Ted climbed out of his sleeping bag and tried to hold Dennis down. At last he lay right across him while Cathy talked to him softly, saying, "Dennis, it's all right. We're right here with you. It's all right, we're here."

Little by little, Dennis got quieter. He was still talking, but they couldn't make out what he was saying. At last he was still.

Ted got up carefully and got back into his sleeping bag and lay down, shaking with the cold. He felt as if he would never warm up. What a night!

Morning came at last, but the storm went right on. The wind howled, the tent shook, the snow rattled against the tent. The storm was as strong as ever.

Ted slept for a while. When he woke up, Cathy gave him a cup of cold oatmeal. "What's this?" Ted asked.

"What do you think it is? It's breakfast! We can't light the stove in here—not with Dennis rolling around like that. So I melted some snow in my sleeping bag and made some oatmeal. Try it! It's nice and sweet."

Ted ate the oatmeal. It made him cold inside, and he was still hungry. "Now, how about some chocolate?" he asked.

"No, I can't let you eat up all the food at once. We don't know how long we will be stuck here, so we have to make the food last. And I have to save some for when Dennis wakes up."

"OK, OK." Ted lay back down again and looked up at the top of the tent. There wasn't anything else to do—he sure didn't feel like talking to Cathy.

Cathy checked to make sure that Dennis was warm, then got back into her sleeping bag and lay down. Without saying a word, she turned her back to Ted.

Ted lay there, listening to the wind howling around the tent and to Dennis and Cathy breathing quietly. Ted was warm inside his sleeping bag. Without knowing it, he fell asleep.

* * * * *

Ted was dreaming.

The snow beat against him, stinging his face. The wind was blowing so hard that he could hardly walk against it. But he had to go on. He had to find that ski pole.

That ski pole again! Ted knew that he was dreaming, and he made himself wake up. He sat up and looked over at the pile of ski poles. His ski poles were there, and Dennis's poles, and Cathy's. They were all there, so he *had* been dreaming again. That nightmare was going to drive him crazy!

He stayed sitting up and tried to think of something to think about. All he could think about was food.

After a while Cathy woke up and said, "Lunch time." She got out two small bits of cheese and a few crackers. She gave one bit of cheese and two crackers to Ted.

Ted spread them out on his lap and looked at them for a while. At last he took a small bite from the cheese. Then he ate a cracker. He wanted to make his lunch last as long as he could.

This was silly! He popped the rest of the cheese and the other cracker into his mouth. At least his mouth was full for a moment.

As he looked around, he saw that the tent seemed

smaller than it had before. "It couldn't be," he thought. "It just feels small because we're stuck in here."

He looked again. It *was* smaller. The snow! The snow was piling up against the sides of the tent, pushing the tent down!

Ted got out of his sleeping bag and put on his boots and his jacket. He pulled on his mittens and tied his scarf around his neck.

"Where do you think you're going?" Cathy yelled.

"I'm going to clear the snow away from the sides of the tent," Ted told her, "and while I'm out there I'm going to check the ropes. Is that all right with you, boss?"

"Be careful! Don't get lost!" Cathy said.

"Don't worry about it." Ted grabbed his snowshoes and crawled out of the tent.

He stood up, and almost fell down again as the wind hit him like a big hand. He could lean against it as if he were leaning against a wall. It took his breath away.

He got down and crawled along the tent, pushing the snow away with his snowshoe. Most of it blew right back in his face, but he kept on. He cleared away as much snow as he could, then put on his snowshoes and walked, one slow step at a time, along the tent rope to the tree. The rope was still tied tightly around the tree, but the tent was pulling hard against it in the wind. "If only it doesn't break," Ted thought.

He turned and looked back at the tent. It was only ten feet away, but he could hardly see it. He could see the path that he had made through the snow, but it was filling in quickly.

He checked the other ropes and then crawled back into the tent. As he cleared the snow from his eyes and face, Cathy watched him quietly. Without saying a word, she handed him a big piece of chocolate.

Ted crawled into his sleeping bag and ate the chocolate in tiny bites. He had never tasted anything so good in his life.

The day passed. Cathy and Ted talked to each other only if they had to. They took turns staying up, one watching Dennis and the other sleeping.

Dennis was lying quietly. Then he started to talk in a low voice. Ted woke Cathy up, and they leaned over Dennis, but they couldn't hear what he was saying.

"He hasn't had anything to eat since yesterday," Cathy said. "That will make him even weaker. Do you think we should try to feed him something?"

"I don't know," Ted said. "He's talking, but he's really asleep. Wouldn't the food make him choke?"

"We'd better try. He's got to keep his strength up."

Cathy made a little bit of oatmeal. She got it as warm as she could, then crawled over to sit beside Dennis. "You hold him up," she told Ted, "and I'll try to feed him." Carefully, Ted lifted Dennis and held him so that he was almost sitting up. Dennis moaned and turned his head against Ted's arm. "Here's some food, Dennis," Cathy said quietly. "You have to eat. Emily and John will be back soon with the rescue team. Till then, you have to keep your strength up." She held a spoonful of oatmeal against Dennis's mouth.

Dennis rolled his head against Ted's arm, but Cathy kept talking to him and holding the spoon against his mouth. At last, without opening his eyes, Dennis ate the spoonful of oatmeal. "He took it! He got it down!" Ted said. "Quick, give him another one!"

Cathy gave Dennis another spoonful of oatmeal, then another. Dennis turned his head away, but Ted carefully turned it back. Cathy got three more spoonfuls of oatmeal into Dennis's mouth. "OK, that's it," she said.

"Let him lie down again. We don't want to give him nightmares again."

"No," Ted said, laying Dennis down on the pad, "not nightmares."

The night came. "We would have been home by now," Ted thought. The city seemed very far away.

In the dark, it was harder to stay awake. At last both Ted and Cathy fell asleep. But if Dennis moved or cried out, they both woke up quickly.

The night passed. Morning came. And the storm went on.

They gave Dennis some more oatmeal with tiny bits of cheese in it. Then Cathy made some cold stew. She gave most of the stew to Ted. Ted saw it, but he was so hungry that he didn't say anything about it.

Later, Ted went out to check the ropes. He cleared away the snow that had piled up against the tent again, then crawled back into the tent. He looked over at Cathy. Would she give him some more chocolate?

Cathy saw his look. "You can't have anything more," she said. "We weren't planning to be out for six days, so our food is getting really low. We have to save some. We can't hike out of here if we're hungry, and we have to save as much as we can for Dennis."

Ted said nothing. He crawled into his sleeping bag and went to sleep.

Another night came. Emily and John had been gone for more than a day. It seemed like forever. It was getting hard for Ted to tell if he was awake or asleep.

Ted was dreaming.

The storm was howling. There was a path through the snow. The path . . . the ski pole—he could see a ski pole . . .

No, now he was awake. The storm was still howling

outside, but he could see the tent above him—it was morning. The ski poles were over there in a pile. Everything was OK. But the storm was still going on. It had gone on for two days. How would the rescue team ever get to them?

The day went by. Cathy and Ted ate a little. Whenever Dennis moved, they lifted him up and fed him as much stew as they could get him to take. Once Ted went out and checked the ropes and cleared away the snow. After that he was so hungry that he felt weak. But most of the time they just slept.

Ted was dreaming.

There was a path through the snow. The snow beat against him, but he had to find the ski pole . . . the ski pole . . .

He woke up. He was getting tired of that nightmare. It was getting to be part of his life. But it wasn't real, he told himself, and just to be sure, he checked the pile of ski poles.

There were only four. Two were gone.

He sat up and looked around the tent. Dennis was there, lying pale and quiet. But where was Cathy?

Her snowshoes were gone, and her jacket. Where was she? What did she think she was doing, going out there without telling him? When *he* went out, Ted always checked with *her!*

He pulled on his boots and jacket and stuck his head out the tent flap. Maybe she was just checking the ropes. "Cathy!" he yelled. "Cathy!" But all he could hear was the howling of the wind.

When the wind dropped for a moment, he could see a path through the snow. It went through the woods to the big meadow.

Where was she? How long had she been gone? Not

too long, or her path would have been filled in with snow by now. But there wasn't any time to lose. He grabbed his hat and tied his scarf around his neck. Then he looked over at Dennis. He didn't want to leave Dennis alone, but he had to go. He put on his snowshoes, grabbed his ski poles, and went out into the snow.

The wind had picked up again, and the snow stung his eyes. Bent down against the wind, he followed the path through the snow.

He came out of the woods and looked out across the big open meadow in front of him. The wind was stronger here, and everything was white. The ground, the sky—it was all white. The path went out into the meadow, but there was no one out there in that world of white.

Where was Cathy? Had she fallen down? Was she somewhere out there under the snow, with more and more snow piling up on her till at last there would be no trace of her—just one big open meadow of snow?

Ted turned and looked back the way he had come. He could see the tent when the wind dropped for a moment, but when he got out into the meadow, it would be easy to get lost. And then Dennis would be alone. Forever.

He needed something to mark the trail back to the tent. He took off his scarf and tied it to a tree by the side of the meadow. Then he set out into the meadow.

He made his way along the path through the snow. He walked out ten feet, then twenty feet. The snow stung his eyes, and the wind pushed against him. But he kept walking.

He looked back. The woods were just a dark line in a white world. The opening in the trees that led to the tent was gone, but he could see the red scarf flapping in the wind.

He walked on. The trail went out into the meadow,

then uphill, then turned and went downhill. Then it went back uphill, and then out into the meadow again. It was clear that Cathy had gotten lost and had been trying to find her way back.

Where was she?

The path through the snow was filling in fast, so it was getting harder and harder to tell where it went. At last Ted stopped. The path was gone. He couldn't follow it anymore.

But he had to go on. He had to go on looking. He had to find her!

He pushed on against the wind. He felt so tired, so sleepy. It would feel so good to lie in the snow and just go to sleep. But he couldn't stop. He had to go on. He had to find—

The ski pole! The ski pole in his nightmare! He could see it! It was over there, sticking out of the snow.

Was he asleep? This was just like his dream. But he knew he was awake. This time it was real.

Ted looked around. The ski pole . . . *where was Cathy?*

The wind blew harder, and some snow blew away. Ted saw something red. It was her jacket.

Ted hurried over to it, threw himself down in the snow, and began to dig. He brushed the snow away from her head. Was she alive?

She moved. She picked up her head and opened her eyes. "Oh, Ted," she said, "I'm so sleepy."

"Get up!" Ted said. "We've got to get you out of here!"

"Oh leave me alone. Let me sleep."

"Do what I say!" Ted shouted, pulling on her arm. "Get up!" He pulled her to her feet and brushed her off. She was beginning to wake up now.

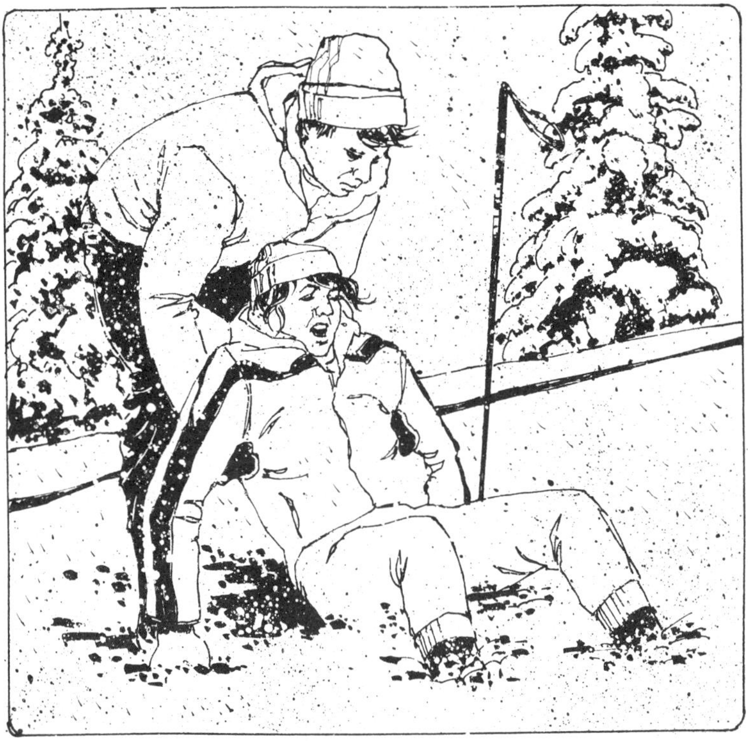

"Oh, Ted," she said, "I thought I heard a plane. I thought the rescue team was out looking for us. So I just came out here to wave to them, to let them know where to find us. But there was no plane, and I got lost. I couldn't find my way back again. I just couldn't think! And then I got so sleepy."

"A plane out in this storm? No way! Come on." Ted looked around. The snow was blowing hard, hiding the woods. He waited for the wind to drop for a moment. There was the scarf! Then it was gone again in the swirling snow. "Come on!" Ted said again as he started to walk to where he had seen the scarf.

The scarf came and went in the blowing snow.

Sometimes they had to stop and wait for the wind to drop so that they could see it again. Without the scarf to guide them, every way seemed the same.

At last they got to the woods and made their way to the tent. The snow was piled deep around it again, but they just crawled in through the tent flap.

Ted helped Cathy take off her snowshoes and boots. He brushed her off with his mittens, then pushed her into her sleeping bag. "I'm sorry, Ted," Cathy said.

"We have to eat more," Ted said. "We've had hardly anything to eat for two days. But we need our strength *now.* We need to eat so that we can stay warm, and so we can think!"

"You're right," Cathy said. She lay down, and in an instant she was asleep.

"We have to think," Ted said again. "We can't do foolish things or we'll all be killed." He looked over at Cathy and saw that she was asleep. "We need rest, too," he added. "I'll just lie down and rest for a moment. In a moment I'll get up and brush the snow off." He pulled his sleeping bag over himself, and he was asleep.

Directions. Answer these questions about the chapter you have just read. Put an *x* in the box beside the best answer to each question.

1. (E) During the storm, what did Ted and Cathy do most of the time?

☐ a. Eat
☐ b. Talk
☐ c. Sleep
☐ d. Ski

2. (A) Cathy said, "I can't let you eat up all the food at once. We have to *make it last.*" What did she mean?

☐ a. She hadn't made the food yet.
☐ b. They had run out of food the night before.
☐ c. She wanted to make a big supper.
☐ d. They had to use the food up as slowly as they could.

3. (E) What was the main thing that Cathy and Ted were worried about in this part of the story?

☐ a. They were afraid that the tent would fall down.
☐ b. They were afraid that Dennis would die before the rescue team found them.
☐ c. They were afraid that they would lose their ski poles.
☐ d. They were afraid to light the stove.

4. (D) Sometimes Ted talked to Dennis. Why?

- ☐ a. He thought that Dennis was awake.
- ☐ b. He wished that his friend were all right.
- ☐ c. He was telling Dennis how to set up the tent.
- ☐ d. He wasn't mad at his friend anymore.

5. (C) What happened right after Ted cleared the snow away from the tent the first time?

- ☐ a. The tent fell down.
- ☐ b. Cathy gave him a piece of chocolate.
- ☐ c. The storm stopped.
- ☐ d. He fed Dennis some oatmeal.

6. (B) Why did Cathy go out into the meadow?

- ☐ a. She thought she heard a rescue plane.
- ☐ b. She wanted to show Ted how strong she was.
- ☐ c. She thought that the storm was over.
- ☐ d. She wanted to try to hike to the city for help.

7. (D) Why did Cathy fall asleep in the meadow?

- ☐ a. She was weak from cold and hunger.
- ☐ b. She was mad at Ted.
- ☐ c. She didn't want to sleep in the tent any longer.
- ☐ d. She wanted to sleep out under the sky.

8. (B) How did Ted find Cathy in the meadow?

- ☐ a. He called to her.
- ☐ b. He heard her moaning.
- ☐ c. He saw her foot sticking out of the snow.
- ☐ d. He saw her ski pole sticking out of the snow.

9. (A) As Ted and Cathy made their way back across the meadow, the scarf *came and went* in the blowing snow. What does that mean?

- ☐ a. Sometimes they could see the scarf, but sometimes it was hidden by the snow.
- ☐ b. First the scarf was there, but then the wind blew it away.
- ☐ c. Sometimes Ted tied the scarf around his neck, but sometimes he left it in his pack.
- ☐ d. First the scarf waved in the wind, then it fell straight down.

10. (C) Which of these things happened last?

- ☐ a. Cathy went out into the meadow.
- ☐ b. Ted got Cathy into her sleeping bag.
- ☐ c. Ted woke up and saw that Cathy was gone.
- ☐ d. Ted found Cathy's ski pole sticking out of the snow.

Skills Used to Answer Questions

A. Recognizing Words in Context B. Recalling Facts
C. Keeping Events in Order D. Making Inferences
E. Understanding Main Ideas

Using Suffixes to Learn New Words

You know that a suffix is a group of letters added to the end of a word to change its meaning. You have learned some common suffixes and their meanings. Review those suffixes and their meanings in the box below:

Suffix	Meaning	Example
-en →	to make →	lighten
-ly →	done in a certain way →	quickly
-ful →	full of →	delightful
-less →	without →	colorless
-ness →	a state of being →	greatness
-able →	able to be →	changeable

Here are some more common suffixes and their meanings:

Suffix	Meaning	Example
-er →	person who →	play<u>er</u>
-ize →	to make →	legal<u>ize</u>
-ward →	moving in some direction →	back<u>ward</u>

By knowing the meanings of suffixes, you can figure out the meanings of some new words you meet as you read.

> To find the meaning of a word with a suffix, follow these steps:
> 1. Find the suffix.
> 2. Try to recall the meaning of the suffix.
> 3. Think about the meaning of the word that the suffix was added to.
> 4. Figure out how the suffix changes the meaning of the word.

For example, maybe you don't know the word *northward*. You can see it has the suffix *-ward*. Think of the word in two parts: *north* and *-ward*. You know that *-ward* means *moving in some direction*. You know that *north* is a direction. So you can guess that *northward* means *moving north*.

What does *eastward* mean?

____

You can do the same with a word such as *hardness*. The suffix, of course, is *-ness*. The word to which the suffix is added is *hard*. You know that *-ness* means *a state of being*. *Hard* means *solid* or *firm*. So you can figure out that *hardness* means *the state of being solid or firm*.

What does *goodness* mean?

____

The suffix *-able* means *able to be.* If you see the word *breakable,* you can think of it in two parts: *break* and *-able.* You can then figure out that *breakable* means *able to be broken.*

What does *readable* mean?

____

Exercise 1

Each word in this exercise has a suffix. Break the word into the suffix and the word that it is added to. Print those two parts on the lines provided. Then, on the last line, print the meaning of the word. The first one has been done for you.

Word with Suffix	**Word**	**Suffix**	**Meaning of Word with Suffix**
1. loudly	loud	ly	done in a loud way
2. smallness	________	____	____________
3. washable	________	____	____________
4. hateful	________	____	____________
5. singer	________	____	____________
6. standardize	________	____	____________
7. darken	________	____	____________
8. backward	________	____	____________

Exercise 2

Below is a list of words with suffixes. Print the meaning of each word on the line beside it. Use the steps for understanding a word with a suffix given on page 147. The first one has been done for you.

1. downward moving down
2. brighten ______________________
3. neatly ______________________
4. hairless ______________________
5. teacher ______________________
6. sorrowful ______________________
7. nearness ______________________
8. punishable ______________________
9. normalize ______________________

Rates for Long Distance Calls: Part Two

Dial-Direct Calls

To make a long distance phone call, you dial *1 + the area code + the telephone number.* You can dial a long distance call yourself. A call that you make without any help from the operator is a *dial-direct call.*

You know that rates for dial-direct calls change with the time of day. Calls made at night cost less than calls made during the day. Calls made late at night or on the weekend are the cheapest calls.

Operator-Assisted Calls

Sometimes you need the operator's help to make a long distance call. A call made with the help of an operator is an *operator-assisted call.* The most common operator-assisted calls are:

1. Public (Coin) Telephone Calls
2. Calling Card Calls
3. Collect Calls

Public (Coin) Telephone Calls. Suppose you are away from home and you must make a long distance phone call from a pay telephone. You will need the operator's help.

To make a long distance call from a pay phone, follow these steps:

1. Dial 0 + the area code + the local number.
2. Wait for the operator to tell you how much money to put in the pay phone.
3. Put the right amount of money in the phone.

Calling Card Calls. Suppose you are away from home and want to make a long distance call. You may want to have the cost of the call charged to your regular phone bill. You can use a *calling card* to make the call. The charge for the call will be put on your monthly phone bill.

A calling card is used to make long distance calls away from home. Calls made with a calling card are billed to your home phone. You can get a calling card free from the phone company. You can use the card to make calls from any phone, including public (coin) telephones.

To make a long distance call with a calling card, follow these steps:

1. Dial 0 + the area code + the local number.
2. Tell the operator you are making a calling card call.
3. Tell the operator your calling card number. The number is printed on your calling card.

Suppose you want to make a calling card call to Fletcher's Department Store. The area code is 418. The phone number is 672-4530.

1. What number will you dial?

____

2. What two things will you tell the operator?

   a. ______________________________

   b. ______________________________

3. When will you pay for the call?

____

Collect Calls. Sometimes when you make a long distance call to a person or a company you want that person or company to pay for the call. In those cases you can call *collect.* When you call collect, the person you call must pay. You need the operator's help to make a collect call.

> To make a collect call, follow these steps:
>
> 1. Dial 0 + the area code + the local number.
> 2. Tell the operator you are making a collect call.
> 3. Give the operator your name.
> 4. When the other party answers, the operator will tell them your name and will ask if they will accept the charges for the call. If they say yes, you can start talking.

Suppose you want to make a collect call to the Acme Carpentry Company. The area code is 313. The phone number is 673-2121.

4. What number will you dial?

____

5. What two things will you tell the operator?

   a. ____

   b. ____

6. Who will pay for the call?

____

Charges for Operator-Assisted Calls

An operator-assisted call costs more than a dial-direct call. You pay the regular long distance rate for a dial-direct call. You know that the regular long distance rate depends on what day and what time you make a call. For an operator-assisted call, you also pay a special charge. The amount of the charge depends on where you live. The extra charges for operator-assisted calls where you live are printed in your local phone book.

A sample list of charges for operator-assisted calls is shown on the following page.

You can see from the list that calling card calls have the lowest special charge. You pay a higher charge for public (coin) phone calls. The charge is highest for collect calls. If you make a calling card call from a public telephone, you pay only the calling card charge.

If you made a calling card call on a weekend, you would pay the regular weekend rate plus the special charge for Calling Card calls.

Suppose you made a long distance call from a public (coin) phone on a weekend, and you paid by putting coins in the phone.

7. What rate and charge would you pay for the call? (Circle your answer.)

   Night and Weekend Rate + .40

   Night and Weekend Rate + .50

   Evening Rate + .50

Calling Card, Operator assistance and coin telephone charges

A separate service charge is added to the intrastate rates when you make the following types of calls **(these charges are never discounted, even for time of day):**

Customer Dialed Calling Card	**$ .40**
Public (coin) Telephones This charge is included in the amount requested for the initial one-minute period.	**$ .50**
Collect Calls	**$1.40**
Operator Person-to-Person	**$2.00**

Rates for Long Distance Calls: Part Two

Dial-direct calls cost less than operator-assisted calls. For an operator-assisted call, you pay the dial-direct rate plus a special charge. The amount charged depends on the kind of call you make. The charge is lowest for calling card calls. You pay more for public (coin) telephone calls. (If you make a calling card call from a pay phone, however, you pay the calling card charge, but not the public phone charge.) Collect calls cost the most.

Exercise 1

Read the description of each phone call below. Look at the rates and charges listed under the description. What rates and charges will you have to pay for each call? Remember—you pay no special charge for dial-direct calls. For each type of operator-assisted call, you pay the dial-direct rate plus a special charge. Circle the correct rate and charge for each call. The first one has been done for you.

1. You make a long distance call on Wednesday at 7 A.M. You use your calling card.

   Night Rate + Calling Card Charge

   Night Rate + Public (Coin) Phone Charge

   Night Rate Only

2. You make a long distance call on Monday at 3 P.M. You call from a pay phone. You do not use your calling card.

   Day Rate + Calling Card Charge

   Day Rate + Public (Coin) Phone Charge

   Day Rate Only

3. You make a long distance call from your home on Thursday at 11:50 P.M. You dial the number yourself. You do not ask the operator for any help.

   Night Rate + Collect Charge

   Night Rate + Public (Coin) Phone Charge

   Night Rate Only

4. You make a long distance call from a pay phone on Tuesday at 8 P.M. The person you are calling pays for the call.

   Evening Rate + Collect Charge

   Evening Rate + Calling Card Charge

   Evening Rate Only

5. You make a long distance call on Saturday at 10:30 A.M. You call from a pay phone and use your calling card.

   Weekend Rate + Public (Coin) Phone Charge

   Weekend Rate + Calling Card Charge

   Weekend Rate Only

Exercise 2

A sample list of special charges for operator-assisted calls is given below.

Calling Card, Operator assistance and coin telephone charges
A separate service charge is added to the intrastate rates when you make the following types of calls **(these charges are never discounted, even for time of day):**
Customer Dialed Calling Card .... **$ .40**
Public (coin) Telephones .... **$ .50** This charge is included in the amount requested for the initial one-minute period.
Collect Calls **$1.40**
Operator Person-to-Person **$2.00**

Use the list to find the special charge you must pay for each of the following calls. Print the amount of the special charge on the line. The first one has been done for you.

1. You make a long distance call from a pay phone. You do not use your calling card.

   Special Charge: $ .50

2. You make a long distance call from a pay phone. You use your calling card.

Special Charge: ____________________

3. You make a long distance call. The call is collect. (The person you are calling will be billed for the call.)

Special Charge: ____________________

4. You make a long distance call from someone's home. You use your calling card.

Special Charge: ____________________

6

Dream of Rescue

Preview Words/*Chapter 6*

Study the words in the box. Then read the sentences below with your teacher. Look carefully at the words in boldface type.

blades	doctor	hugged	splint
burned	faint	leaped	squeezing
cracking	fallen	newspapers	stared
danger	helicopter	please	throat
deathly	hours	sobs	zipper

1. He must have **fallen** asleep.
2. His pants bent with a **cracking** sound.
3. I put your life in **danger**.
4. They should be here in about six **hours**.
5. I'll bet we've been in all the **newspapers**.
6. In six hours, we'll get you to a **doctor**.
7. Ted and Cathy sat and **stared** at him.
8. Oh, **please**, Dennis! You can't be dead!
9. Her body shook with huge **sobs**.
10. I can hear his heart beating. It's very **faint**.
11. He pulled up the **zipper** of the sleeping bag.
12. The flames **leaped** up.
13. His hands grabbed Ted's **throat**.
14. Ted could feel the breath **squeezing** out of him.
15. His face was **deathly** pale.
16. I **burned** it on the stove.
17. We've got to get a **splint** on it to hold it stiff.
18. It's a **helicopter**!
19. He ran to them under the helicopter **blades**.
20. He threw his arms around them and **hugged** them.

Ted slept. He did not dream.

He slept for a long time. When he woke up, it was dark. He was cold—very, very cold.

As he turned over, the cold bit at his legs. Why was he so cold? He reached his arms out, but they didn't touch anything. He wasn't in his sleeping bag! Why not? Then he remembered. He remembered going out to look for Cathy. He remembered getting her back to the tent and getting her into her sleeping bag. But after that he couldn't remember anything.

He had fallen asleep without brushing the snow off. The sleeping bag over him had melted the snow, and then it had slid off him. "Oh no, no!" he thought as he checked his pants. They were frozen so hard that he couldn't even bend his legs. He grabbed his sleeping bag and started to pull it around him. The sleeping bag was wet too. Parts of it were frozen stiff.

Ted began to shake with cold. "Of all the foolish things to do!" he said to himself. "They told me and *told* me not to get wet! And then I go to sleep with snow all over me! My head isn't working any better than Cathy's!"

Now what was he going to do? He was stuck in a tent on a mountain in a snowstorm. He was hungry. And now he was cold, too.

He sat up and tucked his hands under his arms. He banged the toes of his boots against each other. He couldn't feel his toes.

He could hear Dennis breathing quietly. He looked down at him with a worried frown. What would happen to Dennis? How could he and Cathy take care of him if they couldn't think any better than they had been?

Suddenly he noticed that he could hear Dennis's breathing clearly. The wind had dropped!

The storm was over.

Ted moved his legs till his pants bent with a cracking sound. Slowly he crawled over to the tent flap and looked out. The snow was piled up almost to the top of the tent flap, but above the flap he could see the sky. It was clear, and the stars were out.

Ted pushed the soft snow away from the tent flap and climbed out of the tent. He stood up and looked around at the woods, full of clean, white snow. It looked pretty to him, even now. He looked up at the stars sparkling in the clear sky. There were so many of them, far more than he ever saw in the city.

But now he was starting to shake again, so hard that his teeth rattled. He had never been so cold! He put on his snowshoes and walked out along the trail to the meadow. The snow lay deep and smooth, with no marks to show that he and Cathy had ever been there.

He looked up at the mountain. "The wind must really have been something up at the top!" he thought. Then he looked down the mountain at the valley below. He could see lights! Houses! Warm houses with people in them! The lights sparkling in the dark seemed so close, as if he could reach out and touch them.

But they were so far away, so far, far away—part of another world. He had been away from that world for a week. It seemed like forever. Would he ever be part of that world again?

He went back to the tent. He brushed himself off carefully, then crawled in. "Ted, where have you been?"

said Cathy's voice in the dark. "I thought now *you* were lost in the storm!"

"Oh, I'm sorry I scared you. I just went for a walk. The storm is over."

"It is? Why yes, the wind has stopped!" Cathy said. She was quiet for a moment. Then she said, "Ted, I'm really sorry about going out like that. I put your life in danger, and Dennis's life, too. What a fool I was to go out there!"

"You're not the only fool," Ted said, and he told her about his frozen pants and his sleeping bag.

Cathy reached out and touched them. "Oh they *are* frozen!" she said. "You must be cold! Here, you can use my sleeping bag."

"But then *you'll* be cold."

"I'll be all right," Cathy said. She got out of her sleeping bag and started looking in her pack. "Let's have something to eat."

"That sounds good," Ted said. As he got into Cathy's sleeping bag, he started to shake all over. But at last he began to feel warm again.

"Do you remember when we were out in the meadow, when I found you?" he asked Cathy. "You said something about hearing a plane."

"Oh that. I must have been dreaming. You see, I've been dreaming about that plane. I've been dreaming about it over and over, ever since this trip started."

"Really?" Ted asked. "Tell me about it!"

"Well, it started the first night we spent in the tent. I dreamed that I was waiting for something. I didn't know what. I just knew that I had to wait for it. Then the next night, I dreamed that I could hear something—something that sounded like a plane. I waited for it, but I couldn't see it. Every night it's been the same thing. I dream that I'm waiting for a plane. I can hear it, but when I look up into the sky, I can't see it. Then I wake up."

"I've been having a dream too," Ted said. He told her about his nightmare about the ski pole, and about how he had found her by finding the ski pole.

"Wow! Then your dream came true!" Cathy said. "I'm sure glad it did!"

"Maybe *your* dream will come true," Ted said. "Maybe they'll rescue us in a plane."

"Oh no, not in a plane. Where would it land? No, the rescue team will come in the same way we did—on snowshoes. They'll bring a sled for Dennis. They should come today, now that the storm has stopped. They'll start as soon as it gets light, so they should be here by noon. We'll be out before dark."

"You seem to know a lot about it," Ted said. "Have you ever been on a rescue team?"

"Yes, one time. Someone was lost, and a lot of people helped look for him. We looked for more than a week."

"Did you ever find him?" Ted asked.

"No, we never did."

Ted started to shake again. Quickly he said, "Tell me about some of the other trips you've been on."

Cathy told him about the places she had been and the mountains she had climbed. They talked about the places they liked best for camping, and about other things they liked to do. They talked on and on. Suddenly Ted saw that it was getting light. Soon it would be morning.

"The rescue team should be starting out," Cathy said. "They should be here in about six hours. Just six short hours! Then it will be all over! They'll fix up poor old Dennis, and then we'll go home. Home! Hot food! A warm bed! Doesn't that sound good?"

"As soon as I get home, I'm going to take a long, hot bath," Ted said, "and then I'll eat supper. I'll eat everything in my apartment. Then I'll come over to your apartment and I'll eat *you* out of house and home, too!"

"Not if I get there before you," Cathy laughed.

"Then I'll have to call my boss," Ted said. "I've been missing work! She won't know where I've been."

"Oh yes she will," Cathy said. "We've been missing for three days. I'll bet we've been in all the newspapers. Everyone must be worried about us. They don't know if we're alive or dead."

"But we made it!" Ted said. "In six short hours it will be all over." He turned to look at Dennis. "In six hours, we'll get you to a doctor, and . . . Dennis? *Dennis!* Oh God, look at him! I think he's dead!"

In the early morning light, Dennis lay pale and still, so still. Ted and Cathy sat and stared at him. They could not move.

"Dennis, you can't be dead," Cathy said at last. "Not after all you've been through. Just six more hours. Oh please, Dennis, please! You can't be dead!" She put her face in her hands. "We've been sitting here laughing and joking and talking about food, and he . . . he . . ." She began to cry, her body shaking with huge sobs.

Ted put his hands on Dennis's face. Dennis's skin was so cold. But wait, what was that? "Cathy, I think he's breathing!" Ted called.

Cathy crawled over to him. "Really?" she asked between sobs. "Is he really?"

Ted unzipped the two sleeping bags around Dennis

and put his head down on Dennis's chest. Cathy held her breath. A long moment went by. "Yes, I can hear his heart beating!" Ted said. "It's very faint, but it's beating! He's alive! But what are we going to do? He may not last another six hours! What are we going to do?"

"He's too cold!" Cathy said. "We've got to warm him up! Get in the sleeping bag with him and use your own body heat to warm him. The stove might help a little, too. I'll get it going. If only the sun would come up!"

Ted slid into the sleeping bag and lay down next to Dennis. He reached around and pulled up the zipper of the sleeping bag as far as he could. It was such a tight fit that he could hardly breathe.

He could feel Dennis's body next to him, cold and still. Dennis was breathing so slowly and quietly that Ted couldn't hear him. Ted found himself checking over and over to be sure that Dennis's heart was still beating.

The stove started up with a roar that filled the tent. "Be careful," Cathy said. "Don't kick it over." Then she crawled over to Dennis and began to rub his hands.

Carefully, Ted rubbed his face. He tried to will his body heat to go into Dennis. He tried to think warm. He thought about the rescue team, on their way to them with a doctor. Six more hours. No, by now it was just five hours. "Oh, Dennis, don't die!" Ted thought.

Suddenly Cathy leaned over Dennis and said, "Look! He's getting some color back in his face! Is he any warmer?"

"Yes, I think so. He's . . . Hey!"

Dennis moved suddenly. His fist flew up and hit Cathy hard in the face. As Cathy fell over against the side of the tent, Dennis turned on Ted. He hit at Ted's face and neck, shouting, "You can't get me! I'll fight to the end! I'll get you—I'll get all of you!"

Ted tried to grab his arm, but he was so close that he couldn't move. Bang! Bang! The fist slammed down on him again and again. "Oh no you don't!" Dennis shouted. "You won't get me that way!" He kicked out at the tent. "Take that, you stinking rat!"

The stove! Cathy jumped for it and tried to turn it off, but another kick sent her flying. Her arms almost brushed through the flames. Dennis kicked again. The stove tipped and flames leaped up. Cathy threw open the tent flap, grabbed the stove, and threw it out into the snow.

Ted had unzipped the sleeping bag part way, trying to get out. But Dennis threw himself on Ted, shouting, "I'll get you! I'll kill you all!" His hands grabbed Ted's throat. He was so strong! Ted could feel the breath squeezing out of him. He tried to push Dennis away, but he couldn't move him. He couldn't breathe. Everything

was getting black. Was this it? Had he got through that storm just to be killed by his own friend? The rescue team would find them all dead . . .

With one last pull, Ted got his arm free. He reached up and hit Dennis in the face as hard as he could.

Dennis fell like a stone. He lay still, gasping for breath, his face deathly pale. Ted struggled to sit up. "I've killed him!" he gasped.

Then Dennis opened his eyes.

He looked at Ted for a long moment. Then he said softly, "Hey, Ted, you don't look so good."

"Dennis! Dennis! Are you all right? Oh, Dennis!" Ted began to sob.

Dennis tried to sit up. "Ted, what's the matter? Hey, are you all right? What's the matter with you?"

Cathy crawled over to him. "Oh, Dennis!" she said. She threw her arms around him and started to cry.

"What's the matter with you two?" Dennis asked. "Don't let Emily see you like this, or she'll be worried sick. Look at your hand!" he said to Cathy. "What did you do to it?"

"I burned it on the stove," Cathy said. "Don't worry, I'm OK. But how about you—how do you feel?"

"Me? Well, I feel tired, and my leg hurts. Hey, what's going on? I can't move my leg!"

"Don't try to move it," Cathy said. "It's broken."

"Broken! How? What . . ." Dennis tried to ask.

"We've got to get a splint on it to hold it stiff," Cathy went on. "Ted, it's too bad your pants thawed. We could have used them for a splint! Well, we can use Dennis's ski poles. He won't be needing them for a while."

"My ski poles! But . . ."

"Now hold still. I'm going to unzip the sleeping bag all the way. Ted, you get the ski poles."

"Right. I'll get his snowshoes, too. We can use the straps."

"My snowshoe straps! What is going on?" Dennis shouted.

"Just lie down and hold still. We'll tell you all about it," Cathy said. They lay the ski poles down, one on each side of Dennis's leg. Then they took the straps off the snowshoes and strapped the ski poles tightly to his leg. While they worked, they told him everything that had happened since he had fallen from the frozen waterfall.

"Wow!" was all Dennis could say. "I'm sorry!"

"Hey, man, we're just glad you're still with us," Ted told him.

"Now that's a nice splint, if I do say so myself," Cathy said. "Now it's time to get some more food into you. How do you like cold oatmeal? Wait, maybe I can get the stove going again."

"I'll do it," Ted said. "You take care of that burned hand." Ted set up the stove outside. Soon they had a real breakfast of hot tea and hot oatmeal. "This is the best breakfast I've ever had!" Ted shouted over the sound of the stove.

"What a cook!" Cathy laughed.

Suddenly it was quiet as Ted turned off the stove. Then they heard another sound.

Whap—whap—whap—whap . . . The sound was very soft and far away, but it was coming closer. Whap—whap—whap—whap—whap . . .

Cathy crawled out of the tent and stood looking up into the sky. "That's it!" she said. "That's the sound in my dream! The plane is coming!"

"What good will a plane be?" Ted asked as he crawled out of the tent.

"I don't know. But it's coming!"

They stood quietly. The sound came closer. Whap—whap—whap—whap—whap . . .

"That's not a plane!" Ted said suddenly. "It's a helicopter! It's coming up the meadow! Come on!"

Quickly they put on their snowshoes. As they turned back to the tent to grab their ski poles, Dennis was waiting by the tent flap. "You're not going anywhere without me," he said. "I've missed everything in the last three days. I'm not going to miss this."

They carefully pulled him up out of the tent. He put his arms around their necks, and they picked him up between them with his leg sticking out in front. They hurried to the meadow, laughing and gasping for breath.

When they got to the meadow, the helicopter was coming slowly up along the woods. Ted's red scarf was still tied to the branch. Ted untied it and flapped it around his head. Cathy waved her free arm. They all yelled and shouted.

The helicopter came up the meadow. Suddenly it came to them. WHAP—WHAP—WHAP—WHAP—! It hung over them, the huge blades blowing the snow up all around them. Then the helicopter slid away a little and came down till it almost touched the ground. A door popped open and snowshoes stuck out. Then John dropped to the ground. Another man followed him.

"You're all right!" John yelled as he ran to them under the helicopter blades. He threw his arms around them and hugged all three of them at once. "I can't believe it! I never thought I'd see you alive again!"

"Sometimes *we* weren't so sure!" Cathy said.

"Yes, we've had quite a time of it," Ted said.

"Oh don't believe them," Dennis said. "It was nothing, nothing at all. I slept through all of it."

"Where's Emily?" Cathy asked John.

"She's hiking up with the rescue team. But we didn't want to risk taking Dennis down in the sled, not after three days in that storm. We'd better get him in that helicopter."

They carried Dennis to the helicopter. The other man climbed in and pulled Dennis up into the helicopter, being careful not to move his leg. "Cathy, you should go too," Ted said. "You should get a doctor to look at that hand right away."

"Well, OK," Cathy said. "I think I *should* get a ride in the helicopter. After all, I dreamed it up!" The man leaned down and helped her climb in.

"What about you, Ted?" John asked. "They could

squeeze you into the helicopter, too."

"No, I'll stay here and help pack up. I want to walk down." He looked at the sun shining on the new snow. "It's a pretty day for a hike."

The door of the helicopter shut. Then with a roar, the helicopter flew up and moved away down the mountain. John and Ted watched it till it was out of sight. Then they turned and walked back into the snowy woods.

Comprehension Questions*/Chapter 6*

Directions. Answer these questions about the chapter you have just read. Put an *x* in the box beside the best answer to each question.

1. (B) How long did the storm go on?

☐ a. A week
☐ b. Five weeks
☐ c. Three days
☐ d. One day

2. (D) Ted saw more stars when he was on the mountain than he had ever seen in the city. Why?

☐ a. In the city, the stars are hidden by storm clouds.
☐ b. Ted was dreaming when he saw more stars.
☐ c. In the city, other lights shine too brightly for people to see the stars clearly.
☐ d. There are fewer stars over cities.

3. (B) What did Cathy dream about?

☐ a. Waiting for a rescue plane
☐ b. Looking for a ski pole
☐ c. Being lost in the snow
☐ d. Taking care of Dennis

4. (A) Ted told Cathy, "I'll come to your apartment and *eat you out of house and home.*" What did he mean?

- ☐ a. He would eat every bit of her food.
- ☐ b. He would eat supper at her house.
- ☐ c. He would come when she was not at home.
- ☐ d. He would make her get out of her house.

5. (D) Toward the end of the story, Cathy and Ted started talking to each other. Why did they become friends at last?

- ☐ a. They were both happy that Dennis had woken up.
- ☐ b. They both wanted to go in the helicopter.
- ☐ c. They had been through great danger together.
- ☐ d. Emily and John came back and talked them into it.

6. (A) Ted tried to *will* his body heat to go into Dennis. What does *will* mean here?

- ☐ a. Make it happen by thinking about it
- ☐ b. Tell someone what is going to happen
- ☐ c. Write down who will get something when you die
- ☐ d. Take in from somewhere else

7. (C) Which of these things happened last?

- ☐ a. Dennis kicked over the stove.
- ☐ b. Dennis woke up.
- ☐ c. Dennis hit Ted.
- ☐ d. Dennis almost stopped breathing.

8. (E) What was the main thing that Ted proved to Cathy—and himself?

- ☐ a. He knew how to walk on snowshoes.
- ☐ b. His dreams were better than hers.
- ☐ c. He would never learn to be a good winter hiker.
- ☐ d. He had learned to be a good winter hiker.

9. (C) What was the next thing that happened after they heard the helicopter?

- ☐ a. John jumped out of the helicopter.
- ☐ b. Ted made some oatmeal.
- ☐ c. Ted waved his scarf.
- ☐ d. Ted and Cathy carried Dennis to the meadow.

10. (E) What were the two main things that made Ted and Cathy happy in this part of the story?

- ☐ a. The storm stopped and they found some more food.
- ☐ b. Dennis woke up and they were rescued.
- ☐ c. Ted hit Dennis and Dennis woke up.
- ☐ d. Ted saw the lights in the valley and Cathy said she was sorry.

Skills Used to Answer Questions

A. Recognizing Words in Context B. Recalling Facts
C. Keeping Events in Order D. Making Inferences
E. Understanding Main Ideas

Using Suffixes to Make New Words

You know that a suffix is a group of letters added to the end of a word to change its meaning. You have learned how to use suffixes to figure out new words.

Here is a review of the suffixes and meanings you have learned:

Suffix	Meaning	Example
-en →	to make →	lighten
-ly →	done in a certain way →	quickly
-ful →	full of →	delightful
-less →	without →	colorless
-ness →	a state of being →	greatness
-able →	able to be →	changeable
-er →	person who →	player
-ize →	to make →	legalize
-ward →	moving in some direction →	upward

When you know how to add suffixes to words, you can make many new words. For example, suppose you want to make a new word that means *to make deep*. You know that the suffix *-en* means *to make*. Add the suffix *-en* to the word *deep*. You get the new word *deepen*. *Deepen* means *to make deep*.

Exercise 1

Practice making new words by adding suffixes. Below are some words without suffixes. Add a suffix to each word to give it the meaning that is asked for.

To make a new word, follow these steps:

1. Look at the review box of suffixes and meanings above.
2. Find the suffix that has the meaning you need.
3. Add the suffix to the word that is given. Print the new word on the line.

The first one has been done for you.

1. **quiet** (Make a new word that means *done in a quiet way.*)

   quietly ________________

2. **afford** (Make a new word that means *able to be afforded.*)

   ____

3. **dream** (Make a new word that means *person who dreams.*)

   ____

4. **window** (Make a new word that means *without windows.*)

   ____

5. **thank** (Make a new word that means *full of thanks.*)

____

6. **south** (Make a new word that means *moving south.*)

____

Exercise 2

Each sentence below has a word missing. Complete the sentence by making a word with a suffix and printing it in the blank space. The words in dark print after the sentence tell you the meaning of the word that should complete the sentence. To find the suffix you need, look back at the review box of suffixes and meanings at the beginning of this chapter. For help in making the new word, use the steps in Exercise 1. The first one has been done for you.

1. If you do not moisten the back of a stamp, it will not stick. **(to make moist)**

2. I thanked the man for his _______________. **(state of being kind)**

3. The young man greeted the children _______________. **(in a warm way)**

4. Vicki was _______________ by the end of the race. **(without breath)**

5. Al was ________________ that he would get the new job. **(full of hope)**

6. The clown's act was ________________. **(able to be laughed at)**

Important Phone Numbers

At the front of your phone book, you will find a list of important phone numbers. They are the numbers of people or agencies that can help you with problems.

Emergency Numbers

Sometimes you need to get help quickly. You may have an *emergency*. A car accident is an emergency. So is a fire or a sudden illness. You can use your phone to get help quickly in an emergency.

Look inside the front cover of your phone book. *Emergency numbers* are usually listed there. You will find the phone numbers of the police and fire departments. You can call the nearest one for help. Here is a sample of an emergency numbers page:

Emergency Numbers

fire	dial	police	dial
Chicago Heights	754-2121	Chicago Heights	754-2121
Crawford Countryside	798-3161	Crawford Countryside	458-1000
Crete	672-7221	Crete	672-7241
East Chicago Heights	758-3451	East Chicago Heights	758-3441
Glenwood	758-2121	Glenwood	758-2131
Holbrook	754-4121	Holbrook	458-1000
Lynwood	758-2321	Lynwood	758-6100
Matteson	748-5121	Matteson	748-5131
Miller Woods	758-7787	Miller Woods	458-1000
Olympia Fields	748-5121	Olympia Fields	748-2131
Olympia Gardens	755-1616	Olympia Gardens	458-1000
Park Forest	748-5151	Park Forest	748-5151

The local police and fire departments are listed in alphabetical order. Call the one that is closest to you.

Suppose you are in Glenwood. You see a house that is on fire. Look under *fire* on the emergency numbers page. Call the number for the Glenwood Fire Department.

1. What is the number for the Glenwood Fire Department?

   ____

2. What number would you call if someone robbed your home in Glenwood?

   ____

3. What number would you call to report a fire in Park Forest?

   ____

Helpful Numbers

Sometimes you may need help with a problem that is not an emergency. For example, you may need help in looking for a job. You may need help to figure out your taxes. You may have a question about your social security. You may need help in reading legal papers.

The phone company lists the phone numbers of places that can help you with problems like those. You will find those numbers listed on a special page. In some phone books this page is called *Helpful Numbers.* In other phone books it is called *Community Service Numbers.* In still others it is called *Easy Reference List of Public Services.*

The special page of service numbers is at the front of many phone books. Some books place it at the beginning of the blue pages section. In your own phone book, find the page that lists places that can help you with problems. Here is a sample of such a page:

Helpful Numbers

Alcoholism

Alcoholics Anonymous	346-1475
South Suburban Council on Alcoholism	
Harvey	333-4357
Park Forest	481-9310
Park Forest	747-1234

Ambulance

See "Ambulance Service" in Yellow Pages

Automobiles

Licenses: See "Licenses"	
Registrations, titles	481-4310

Birth and Death Certificates

Cook County	443-7790

Health Care

Cook County Department of Public Health	
Harvey	333-0006
Crisis Intervention and Suicide Prevention	
Illinois Mental Health Dept.	794-3609
Illinois Public Aid Medical	
Assistance	326-5400
Venereal Check List (toll-free)	800 252-8989
Will County Health Department	
Park Forest South	534-0800

Hospitals

Ingalls Memorial (Harvey)	333-2300
St. James (Chicago Heights)	756-1000
South Suburban (Hazel Crest)	799-8000

Housing

Cook County Housing Authority	939-0742
Chicago Heights	757-4640
Robbins	388-3892
U.S. Housing and Urban	
Development	353-5880

Income Tax

Federal (toll-free)	800 972-5400
State of Illinois	641-2150

The words in dark print are the names of things you might have problems with. Those words, called *headings,* are in alphabetical order. The phone numbers of places that can help you with problems are listed under the words in dark print.

When you need help with a problem, follow these steps:

1. Turn to the page in your phone book that lists service or helpful numbers.
2. Look over the headings—the words in dark print. Find the name of the problem you want help with.
3. Look at the list of places under that name.
4. Find the phone number of the place that will help you most.

4. Suppose you want to find out how to register your automobile. Look under the heading **Automobiles**. Find the number for *Registrations*. What is the number?

____

5. Suppose you need help on your state income tax. What heading would you look under?

____

What number should you call?

____

Finding Helpful Numbers

You know that you can use the phone book to get help when you need it. Below is a list of helpful numbers:

Exercise 1

Use the list to answer the following questions. The first one has been done for you.

1. You live in Sauk Village. You want to get a library card.

   a. What heading (word in dark print) do you look for?
   Libraries

   b. What place do you call? Sauk Village

   c. What number do you call? 757-4771

2. You smell gas coming from your stove.

   a. What heading do you look for? ______________

   b. What place do you call? ______________

   c. What number do you call? ______________

Helpful Numbers

Alcoholism
- Alcoholics Anonymous 346-1475
- South Suburban Council on Alcoholism
  - Harvey 333-4357
- Park Forest 481-9310

Ambulance
- See "Ambulance Service" in Yellow Pages

Automobiles
- Licenses: See "Licenses"
- Registrations, titles 481-4310

Birth and Death Certificates
- Cook County 443-7790

Gas Leaks
- Northern Illinois Gas
  - Chicago Heights 756-5100

Government Agencies—Information
- Cook County 443-3390
- Federal Information Center 353-4242
- Governor's Action Office 793-3757

Insurance Complaints
- Illinois Department of Insurance ... 793-2427

Legal Aid
- Chicago Heights Service Center 754-4575
- Cook County Public Defender
  - Markham 331-0933
- Legal Assistance Foundation
  - Harvey 339-5550

Libraries
- Chicago Heights 754-0323
- Park Forest 748-3731
- Richton Park 481-5333
- Sauk Village 757-4771
- Steger—South Chicago Heights 755-5040

Licenses
- Automobile (information) 481-4310
- Driver's license exam 481-4310
- Marriage license 443-5663

Sewers
- Chicago Heights 754-0254
- Olympia Fields Public Works 747-8286
- Park Forest 748-1112
- Richton Park Sewerage Plant 748-1288
- Steger Public Works 755-3888

Social Security Administration
- Harvey 333-1140

3. You want to get a marriage license.

a. What heading do you look for? ____________

b. What place do you call? ____________

c. What number do you call? ____________

4. You live in Park Forest. The sewer on your street is clogged.

a. What heading do you look for? ____________

b. What place do you call? ____________

c. What number do you call? ____________

To the Instructor

Purpose of the Series

Teachers charged with the responsibility of providing instruction for adults and older students with reading difficulties face a major problem: the lack of suitable materials. Stories written at the appropriate level of maturity are too difficult; stories easy enough to read independently are too childish.

The stories in the Adult Learner Series were written to solve the readability problem. The plots and characters in these stories are suitable for adults and older students, yet the stories can be read easily by very low-level readers.

The principal goal of the series is to provide interest and enjoyment for these readers. To this end, every attempt has been made to create a pleasant reading experience and to avoid frustration. The plots move quickly but are kept simple; a few characters are introduced and developed slowly; the same characters are utilized throughout a text; sentence structure and vocabulary are carefully monitored.

A secondary goal is to help adults explore and develop everyday life skills. Lessons and exercises about a variety of life skills provide adults and older students with the basic competencies they need for success in this fast-paced world.

Rounding out the structure of the series are exercises for developing vocabulary skills, comprehension skills, and language skills.

Reading Level

The stories in the Adult Learner Series are all written at second and third grade reading levels. It should be kept in mind, however, that the stories were written for adults: people with a wider range of experience and larger speaking and listening vocabularies than those of elementary school children. Thus, there are some words and some events which might present difficulties for elementary school students but which should not pose problems for older beginning readers.

Besides the slightly increased complexity of vocabulary and plot, the writing style itself has been adapted for older beginning readers. Every effort was made to make the prose sound natural while maintaining simplicity of structure and vocabulary. The repetition of words and phrases has been carefully controlled to permit maximum learning of new words without producing a childish effect.

The reading level of the stories was established by applying Dr. Edward B. Fry's *Formula for Estimating Readability* and *3,000 Instant Words* by Elizabeth Sakiey and Edward Fry. *3,000 Instant Words* lists the 3,000 most common words in the English language, ranked in order of frequency. The first 100 words on the list and their common variants [*-s, -ing,* etc.] make up 50 percent of all written material. The first 300 words and their variants make up 65 percent of all written material. Because readers encounter a relatively small number of words so frequently, they must be able to recognize the Instant Words immediately to be effective readers.

The story line of *Nightmare Snow* presents some situations—problems and techniques of facing the elements in winter mountaineering—which may be new to some students. For them, and perhaps for all students, a discussion of these concepts might improve comprehension and enhance the element of reading for pleasure which is the primary purpose of all the stories in the Adult Learner Series.

Structure and Use of the Text

Each book in the Adult Learner Series is divided into several units. Each unit follows a regular format consisting of these sections:

Preview Words

Twenty words from each chapter are presented for students to preview before reading. Those words that were expected to give students the most difficulty were chosen for previewing. The preview section includes all words of more than one syllable that are not among the first 2,000 words on Sakiey and Fry's list of 3,000 Instant Words. The words are listed first in alphabetical order and then shown again in story sequence in sentences based on the chapter.

The twenty sentences match the chapter in readability; students can read the sentences independently. With some classes the instructor may want to read the words and sentences aloud for students to repeat and learn. In very structured classes, the words could also be used for spelling and writing practice.

Story

The primary purpose of the story is to provide interesting material for adult readers. It should be read as a story; the element of pleasure should be present. Because of the third grade reading level, students should be able to read the story on their own.

Comprehension Questions

Ten multiple-choice comprehension questions follow each chapter. There are two questions for each of these five comprehension skills:

A. Recognizing Words in Context
B. Recalling Facts
C. Keeping Events in Order
D. Making Inferences
E. Understanding Main Ideas

The letters *A* through *E* appear in the text as labels to identify the questions.

The comprehension questions are constructed to cover all parts of the chapter evenly and to bring out important points in the story. This insures that the student understands the story so far before going on to the next chapter.

Students should answer the questions immediately after reading the chapter and correct their answers using the key at the back of the book. Students should circle incorrect responses and check off correct ones.

The graphs at the back of the book help the instructor keep track of each student's comprehension progress. The *Comprehension Progress Graph* shows comprehension percentage scores. The *Skills Profile Graph* identifies areas of comprehension weakness needing special attention and extra practice.

Language Skills

These sections cover many aspects of language study: phonics, word attack skills, simple grammar, and correct usage. The readability of these sections is higher than that of the chapters. The readability level varies depending on the vocabulary load of the specific language skill being taught.

Because the language skills are taught in clear and simple terms, most students will be able to work these sections independently. However, the instructor should be alert for opportunities to explain and further illustrate the content of the lessons.

The lessons contain exercises which give students the opportunity to practice the language skills being taught. An answer key at the back of the book makes it possible for students to correct their work.

Understanding Life Skills

Every chapter is accompanied by two sections which deal with life skills. The first, "Understanding Life Skills," introduces and fully explains a specific life skill. The life skills all revolve around some detail of modern adult life.

Because this section stresses *understanding* a certain life skill, the reading level is higher than the reading level of the story. However, the life skill lessons are presented in carefully prepared steps, and most students should be able to read and comprehend them without too much difficulty.

Questions used in the lessons are designed to focus the students' attention and to reinforce the learning. Answers for all questions are provided at the back of the book.

Applying Life Skills

Because modern-day living requires both *knowing* and *doing,* two life skills sections follow each chapter to emphasize both aspects. The second, "Applying Life

Skills," is primarily a practical exercise.

This section builds on the understanding generated in the previous section. Students should be able to complete the exercise successfully by applying what they have just read.

Completing this section allows students to demonstrate their mastery of a specific life skill. It gives them the firsthand experience they need with tasks they are likely to encounter in everyday living.

An Answer Key at the back of the book helps students correct their work and gives them immediate feedback.

All units in each book are structured alike, each consisting of the six sections described here. Students quickly discover the regular pattern and are able to work with success and confidence throughout the text.

Use in Small-Group or Class Situations

Although the books in the Adult Learner Series were designed primarily for use on an individual basis, they can be used successfully in small-group or class situations. The comprehension, language and life skills questions can be adapted to whole-class instruction; this may be especially useful for students of English as a Second Language. If several students have read the stories, a group discussion may prove rewarding as well as motivating.

Writing Assignments

The comprehension questions and answers may also serve as suggestions for writing assignments.

For many students at this level, a writing assignment must be introduced in a very structured manner;

otherwise, some students may find themselves unable to get started. On a group basis, the writing assignment may grow naturally out of the class discussion. In this case, the discussion may be all the introduction necessary.

On an individual basis, however, and also often within a group situation, it will be necessary to provide the student with a more concrete starting point. The teacher may find it necessary to provide model sentences or paragraphs, or to supply sentence beginnings ("If I had been there, I would have . . .") for the student to complete. The students can use their copies of the stories to search for word spellings, or the teacher may wish to write suggested words on the blackboard or provide a prepared list.

The Word List

Every word used in the story is included in the Word List, given alphabetically under the chapter in which it is first introduced. New forms that are made by adding the suffixes *-s, -ed, -ing,* and *-ly* to words that have already been introduced are indented.

The instructor may wish to scan the Word List to choose preview words in addition to the twenty in the Preview Words section at the beginning of each chapter. Non-phonetic words, which may present some difficulties in decoding, are printed in italics for quick identification.

The Word List may also be used for the study of common sight words. Since an effort has been made to provide adequate repetition of each word, most of these words should be a solid part of the student's sight vocabulary by the time he or she has finished reading the story.

Summary of the Chapters in Nightmare Snow

Chapter 1: Too Big to Move (Level 3.1)

Ted dreams that he is lost in the snow, searching for something—he doesn't know what—and increasingly tempted to lie down and sleep. Although he feels that the dream may be a warning, he allows his friend Dennis to talk him into joining a winter backpacking trip. Dennis helps him to put together the necessary equipment, and the group sets off.

Chapter 2: Buried Alive! (Level 3.5)

Ted finds his first day of backpacking on snowshoes difficult but fun. The group loses the trail and spreads out to search for markers. Ted steps on a pine tree which has been bent down by the snow and is buried when it springs up beneath him. Eventually the others find him and dig him out. They push on and make camp by a waterfall.

Chapter 3: A Mountain is Full of Surprises (Level 3.7)

Ted's nightmare recurs. The next day the group climbs further up the mountain, making camp just below the tree line. On the third day, after Cathy has been nearly blown away by the high winds, they reach the top.

Chapter 4: The Nightmare Begins (Level 3.1)

The trip down on a packed trail goes quickly. The group gets back to the waterfall with time to spare, so they decide to make camp early and explore. Dennis falls from the waterfall, is knocked unconscious, and goes into shock. John and Emily go for help while Ted and Cathy make camp and try to care for Dennis in an on-coming blizzard.

Chapter 5: The Ski Pole (Level 3.4)

The blizzard rages for three days. The food runs out. Cathy and Ted talk little, sleeping most of the time; Ted slips in and out of his nightmare. Dennis is still unconscious, sometimes raving. Ted wakes up and finds Cathy gone. He searches for her, his nightmare comes true, and gets her back to the tent.

Chapter 6: Dream of Rescue (Level 2.9)

Ted wakes up and finds his clothes frozen, but the storm is over. He and Cathy talk about what they will do when they get home until they see that Dennis is near death. They get him warmed up, and he suddenly attacks them in a fit of delirium. He regains consciousness at last. A helicopter comes to take them away.

Words Introduced in the Story

Non-phonetic words are in italics. New forms of words already introduced are indented.

Chapter 1: Too Big to Move

- a
- able
- about
- across
- after
- *again*
- *against*
- *ahead*
- air
- *all*
- *almost*
- along
- *already*
- am
- and
- *another*
- *any*
- *anything*
- apartment
- *are*
- *aren't*
- around
- as
- asked
- at
- away

- back
- backpack
  - backpacks
- bad
- bag
  - bags
- bang
- bare
- be
  - being
- beat
- became
- because
- bed
- *been*
- before
- began
- believe
- beside
  - besides
- best
- bet
- big
  - bigger
- black
- blew
- blowing
- blowout
- book
- boots
- boxes
- *breakfast*
- *brought*
- but
- by
- call
  - called
- came
- camp
  - camping
- can
- can't
- car
  - cars
- care
- carry
- catch
- Cathy
  - Cathy's
- chair
- change
  - changed
- chapter
- chin
- city
- clean
- clear
- *climbed*
- clock
- coat
- *cold*
- *come*
  - *coming*
- cooking
- corner
- *could*

couldn't
course
cover
crazy
cross
cut

day
days
deep
Dennis
didn't
die
dirty
do
doing
does
done
don't
door
down
dream
dreaming
dressed
drove

early
eat
eating
else
Emily
enjoying
even
ever
every
everybody
everyone
everything
everywhere
excited
extra
eyes

face
fall
far
fat
fear
feel
feeling
feet
felt
few
fifty
fighting
filled
find
fine
first
five
flat
floor
food
fool
for
forgot
fresh
friend
friends
from
front
frostbite
frown
frozen
fun

get
getting
girl
girls'
glad
go
going
gone
good
got
grabbed
great
grinned
grinning
groaned
ground

had
hand
hands
happen
happened
happy
hardly
has
hat
hate
hated
have
haven't
he
he'll
he's
head
hear
heard
heavy
held

help
  helped
here
  here's
hi
hiker
  hiking
him
himself
his
hit
holding
home
hope
how
  how's
hung
hurry
  hurried

I
  I'm
  I've
  I'll
ice
if
in
inside
into
is
isn't
it
  it's

jack
  jacked
jacket
  jackets

John
jokes
jumped
just

keep
kicked
kid
  kidding
  kids
knew
knotting
know
  knows

laid
last
late
  lately
  later
lay
leaned
  leaning
leaving
let
  let's
lie
lifted
light
like
little
long
look
  looked
lose
lost
lot
  lots

love
lovely
lucky
lunch

made
make
map
matter
maybe
me
meadow
mean
meet
mess
Mickey Mouse
  Mickey Mouse's
middle
might
mind
minute
mitten
  mittens
more
morning
mountain
move
much
must
my

neck
need
never
new
next
nice
night

nights
nightmare
nightmares
no
not
nothing
noticed
now
nuts

of
off
oh
OK
on
once
one
onto
open
opened
or
other
others
our
out
over

pack
packed
pair
party
passed
people
pick
picked
piled
place
places

planning
pointed
pointing
poles
pots
pounds
pretty
problem
protect
puffed
pull
pulled
pulling
push
pushed
put
putting

quick
quickly
quiet
quite

read
ready
real
really
remember
remembered
rent
rest
right
road
roll
roof
room
rubbed
rubber

rug
run
running

said
same
sang
sat
saw
say
saying
says
scare
seat
see
seem
seemed
seen
set
shake
shaking
share
shared
she
shining
shook
should
shouted
shouting
show
side
sidewalk
sign
signs
silly
since
sit
sixty

ski
skidded
sky
slammed
sleep
  sleeping
slid
slowly
small
smiled
snow
  snowy
snowshoes
so
soft
some
someone
something
somewhere
songs
soon
sound
spare
sparkles
spun
stairs
standing
start
  started
station
stepped
still
stood
stop
  stopped
store
story
stoves

strap
street
  streets
string
stuff
such
suddenly
Sue
summer
sun
supper
sure

take
  takes
talk
  talking
  talked
Ted
  Ted's
tell
  telling
tent
  tents
than
that
  that's
the
their
them
then
there
  there's
these
they
  they'd
  they're
thick

thing
  things
think
third
this
those
thought
three
through
tightly
till
time
  times
tire
  tired

to
told
tomorrow
too
took
top
trail
trip
  trips
try
  tried
  trying
turn
  turned
two

under
up
us
use
  used

very

wait
waited
waiting
wagon
walk
walked
walks
wall
want
wanted
warm
was
wasn't
watch
waterfall
waved
way
we
we'll
we're
wear
weather
well
went
were
wet
what
what's
wheel
when
where
while
white
who
why
will
wind
windy
window
winter
with
without
woke
wonder
won't
woods
work
worked
working
worry
would
wrong

years
yes
you
you'll
you're
you've
your
yourself

Chapter 2: Buried Alive!

above
afraid
afternoon
alive
alone
anyway
apart
arms
ask
asleep
ate

bar
bare
because
begin
behind
bending
better
between
bird
bit
bits
blow
blue
body
boss
branch
branches
break
breaking
breathing
brightly
broke
brush
brushed
bump
buried
busy

careful
carefully
carried
cheese
chocolate
climb
close
clothes
colors
covered
crackers
crooked
crossly
crowded
cup
cups

dark
death
deeper
Dennis's
did
different
digging
doesn't
doing
dripping
dug

each
ears
easier
eaten
end
ended

falling
fast
faster
fell
finished
flash
flashlight
follow
followed
following
foot
footprints
forget
found
freeze
funny

gap
gave
give
goes

hadn't
handed
hands
hanging
happily
hard
hat
having
her
hey
hiked
hill
hit
hold
holding
holds
hole
hop
hot
hungry
hurt

I'd

kept
kick

left
life
lift
line
listened
listening
longer
looking
looks
loose
loud
low
lower
lying

makes
marked
markers
melt
melted
miss
moment
most
mouth
moved
moving

near

numb

ones
only
ourselves
own

packing
packs
parking
peaceful
pep
person
pictures
piece
pile
pine
pink
pocket
pole
popped
pot
prettier
push
pushing

rabbit
rats
reached
rubbed

sandwich
sank
save
saved
seems
setting
seventy
shadows
shake
shone
short
shouldn't
shout
showed
singing
sink
slipped
slow
slowest
slowly
smelled
smile
smooth
snowshoe
soft
softly
sometimes
space
sparkled
sparkling
spilled
split
spoon
spooned
spooning
sprang
spread
spring
stamp
stand
stars
starting
stay
stayed
steadily
steam
step
steps
stew
sticking
stirring
stop
straining
strange
stuck
stuffed
stumbled
stung
sunlight
sweat
swung

taking
taken
thank
thanks
they'll
thinking
thoughts
thrashed
tied
tiny
tiring
tip
toes
track
tracks
tree
trees
tucked
turns

unless

using

voice
voices

walking

watching
water
wave
we'd
we've
where's

whole
wide
wished
world
worried
wouldn't

Chapter 3: A Mountain is Full of Surprises

always
awake

backs
banged
below
best
birds
blindly
blown
boiling
both
breath
broke
bustled

calling
cameras
cares
climbing
closely
cloud
color
cook
cooked
cooks
crawled
crawling
crossed

diamonds
dreamed

ear
easy
edge
everything's

faded
farther
feeling
fifteen
finally
flew
fly
folded
forever
free
full
fully

gasping
gets
gleamed
grew
grow

hamburger
hang
harder
high
higher
hopping
horizon
howled

its
itself

John's

keeping
knocked

laughed
laughing
least
lighter
liked
lit

making
mile
miles
minutes
missed
mix
mixed
Mom
mountains

nibbled

oatmeal
outlined
outside

packed
painfully
pale
part
path
picture
piles
pushes

quietly

ran
reminded
rice
ridge
risk
roads
rock
rocks
rocky
rolled

scared
searching
second
shoelaces
shook
shoulder
shoulders
shut
sides
sideways
sleepily
slippery
smells
sniffed
snows
sometime
sorry
spend
stared
steeper
stiff
stove
straps
strong
struggled
struggling
surprises

tea
threw
tie
today
together
tonight
tops
toward
towns
turning
twenty
twisted

unzipped

waist
wants
warmed
watched
weren't
wildly
worth

yelled
you'd

zipped

Chapter 4: The Nightmare Begins

ago
aid
anyone
arm

begins
bend
blinding
broken

bumped

camera
camped
chances
cloth
clouds
cloudy
comes
covering
cry
cried
crying

drive
dropped

Emily's

feels
fingers
flap
flapped
flapping
flying
four
fourth

gasped
gasps
gear
God
grab

happens
hid
hide
hike
hikers
hitting
hood
howling

keys
kit

leave
leg
lighter
luck
lunches

mad
matches
may
melting
moan

needs

old

pad
patted

quite

rattled
rescue
rope

screamed
shock
sitting
slide
sliding
slip
slipping
snowman
sounded
squatting
starts
steep
storm
strongest
swimming

team
thin
tighter
tying

valley

wake
waving
which
worrying

yet

Chapter 5: The Ski Pole

added
beginning
bite
bites
check
checked
choke
cleared
cracker
daytime
downhill
drop
fed
feed
filling
foolish
guide
hasn't
hiding
killed
knowing
lap
laying
lean
led
mark
moaned
needed
opening
passed
piling
plane
planning
quieter
red
ropes
scarf
shape
six
sleepy
slept
smaller
sooner
spoonful
spoonfuls
staying
stinging
strength
stronger
sweet
swirling
tasted
ten
trace
uphill
wakes
waking
weak
weaker
whenever
word
yesterday

Chapter 6: Dream of Rescue

anywhere
bath
beating
bet
blades
bring
brushing
burned
checking
chest
clearly
closer
cracking
danger
dead

deathly
doctor
dove

faint
fallen
fight
fist
fit
fix

helicopter
hours
house
houses
huge
hugged
hurts

joking

kicked
kill
killed

land
leaped

legs
lights

man
many
myself

necks
needing
newspapers
noon

pants
parts
please
poor

reach
ride
roar
rub

sent
skin
sled
snowstorm
sob

sobs
sounds
spent
splint
squeeze
squeezing
stinking
stone
strapped

teeth
throat
tight
tipped
touch
touched
true

unzip

warmer
way
week
whap

zipper

Answer Key

Comprehension Questions

Chapter 1

1. c	2. b	3. b	4. a	5. a
6. d	7. a	8. b	9. d	10. c

Chapter 2

1. b	2. b	3. d	4. c	5. c
6. b	7. a	8. c	9. a	10. d

Chapter 3

1. d	2. a	3. b	4. c	5. b
6. c	7. a	8. c	9. c	10. b

Chapter 4

1. a	2. b	3. b	4. d	5. a
6. c	7. b	8. c	9. b	10. b

Chapter 5

1. c	2. d	3. b	4. b	5. b
6. a	7. a	8. d	9. a	10. b

Chapter 6

1. c	2. c	3. a	4. a	5. c
6. a	7. b	8. d	9. d	10. b

Language Skills

Chapter 1: Exercise 1

1. inter
2. un
3. pre
4. mis
5. re
6. un
7. mis
8. pre
9. re

Exercise 2

1. unsure
2. antifreeze
3. rerun
4. prewashed
5. unsafe
6. intercity
7. misfired

Exercise 3

1. before war
2. heat again
3. use wrong
4. against war
5. use again
6. heat before

Chapter 2

not pleasant, not nice
half circle

Exercise 1

1. semi	formal	half formal
2. un	tidy	not tidy
3. mis	understand	understand wrong
4. pre	view	view before
5. sub	human	below human
6. non	sense	not sense
7. inter	change	change between

Exercise 2

1. not ordered
2. light again
3. half sweet
4. treat wrong
5. not a worker
6. not honest
7. against cancer

Chapter 3

recook

Exercise 1

1. replant
2. premixed
3. subsurface
4. repave
5. antitheft
6. misread
6. interweave

Exercise 2

1. misspelled
2. reread
3. mispronounced
4. antirust
5. preseason
6. subzero
7. semiprivate

Chapter 4: Exercise 1

1. en
2. ly
3. less
4. ful
5. able
6. ness

Exercise 2

1. hatless
2. wearable
3. sweeten
4. goodness
5. painful
6. smoothly

Exercise 3

1. to make damp
2. state of being mild
3. able to be returned
4. state of being damp
5. without harm
6. state of being weak
7. able to be inhabited
8. full of harm
9. to make weak
10. done in a mild way

Chapter 5

moving east
state of being good
able to be read

Exercise 1

1. loud	ly	done in a loud way
2. small	ness	state of being small
3. wash	able	able to be washed
4. hate	ful	full of hate
5. sing	er	person who sings
6. standard	ize	to make standard
7. dark	en	to make dark
8. back	ward	moving back

Exercise 2

1. moving down
2. make bright
3. done in a neat way
4. without hair
5. person who teaches
6. full of sorrow
7. state of being near
8. able to be punished
9. to make normal

Chapter 6: Exercise 1

1. quietly
2. affordable
3. dreamer
4. windowless
5. thankful
6. southward

Exercise 2

1. moisten
2. kindness
3. warmly
4. breathless
5. hopeful
6. laughable

Understanding Life Skills

Chapter 1

1. Esther
2. 334 Dionne St Montvl
3. 529-4427
4. Ancone Linda
   Anderson Arthur E
5. Anderson J
6. before

Chapter 2

1. 301
2. 716
   518
3. 1 + 617 + 965-1584

Chapter 3

1. 1 + 804 + 555-1212
2. Richmond
3. Margaret Hill, 54 Oak Street

Chapter 4

1. Day Rate
2. Night and Weekend Rate
3. Night and Weekend Rate
4. Evening Rate

Chapter 5

1. 0 + 418 + 672-4530
2. a. I am making a calling card call.
   b. The number on my calling card
3. It will be on my next phone bill.
4. 0 + 313 + 673-2121
5. a. My name
   b. This is a collect call.
6. Acme Carpentry Company
7. Night and Weekend Rate +.50

Chapter 6

1. 758-2121
2. 758-2131
3. 748-5151
4. 481-4310
5. Income Tax 641-2150

Applying Life Skills

Chapter 1: Exercise 1

1. 884-8590
2. 944-0789
3. 695-0009
4. 699-7806

Exercise 2

1. 31 Privet Pawt
2. 50 Arnold Rd Cov
3. Peeptoad Rd N Scit
4. 88 Doyle Av Prov

Exercise 3

1. Arnold Rd
2. 941-1105
3. Crns
4. 50 Murray Cov

Chapter 2: Exercise 1

1. 313
2. 702
3. 918
4. 601
5. 415

Exercise 2

1. 1 + 601 + 468-4542
2. 1 + 315 + 683-6495
3. 1 + 804 + 528-6743
4. 1 + 406 + 721-8163

Chapter 3: Exercise 1

1. 411
2. 1 + 402 + 555-1212
3. 411
4. 1 + 406 + 555-1212
5. 1 + 201 + 555-1212

Exercise 2

1. Dallas
   John P. Greene, 15 Ivy Street
2. Ithaca
   Maria Garcia, 98 Lookout Drive
3. Harrisburg
   Shady Top Motel
4. Sacramento
   Sears-Roebuck

Chapter 4

1. Evening Rate
2. Night and Weekend Rate
3. Day Rate
4. Night and Weekend Rate
5. Day Rate
6. Evening Rate
7. Evening Rate
8. Night and Weekend Rate

Chapter 5: Exercise 1

1. Night Rate + Calling Card Charge
2. Day Rate + Public (Coin) Phone Charge
3. Night Rate Only
4. Evening Rate + Collect Charge
5. Weekend Rate + Calling Card Charge

Exercise 2

1. .50   2. .40   3. 1.40   4. .40

Chapter 6

1. a. Libraries
   b. Sauk Village
   c. 757-4771
2. a. Gas Leaks
   b. Northern Illinois Gas, Chicago Heights
   c. 756-5100
3. a. Licenses
   b. Marriage license
   c. 443-5663
4. a. Sewers
   b. Park Forest
   c. 748-1112

Comprehension Progress Graph

How to Use the Comprehension Progress Graph

1. At the top of the graph, find the number of the chapter you have just read.
2. Follow the line down until it crosses the line for the number of questions you got right.
3. Put a dot • where the lines cross.
4. The numbers on the other side of the graph show your comprehension score.

For example, this graph shows the score of a student who answered 7 questions right for Chapter 1. The score is 70%.

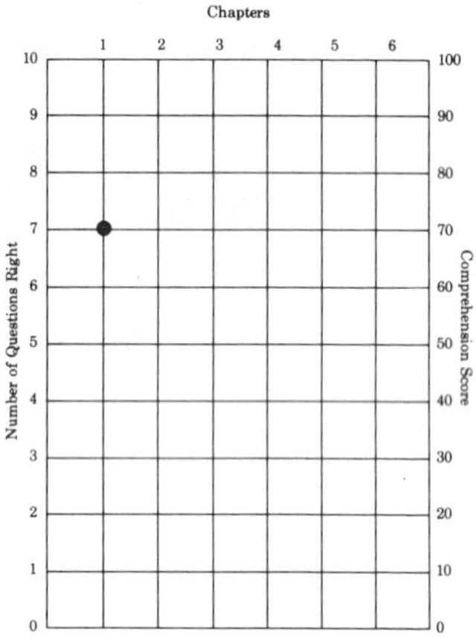

This same student got scores of 80% and 90% on Chapters 2 and 3. The line connecting the dots keeps going up. This shows that the student is doing well.

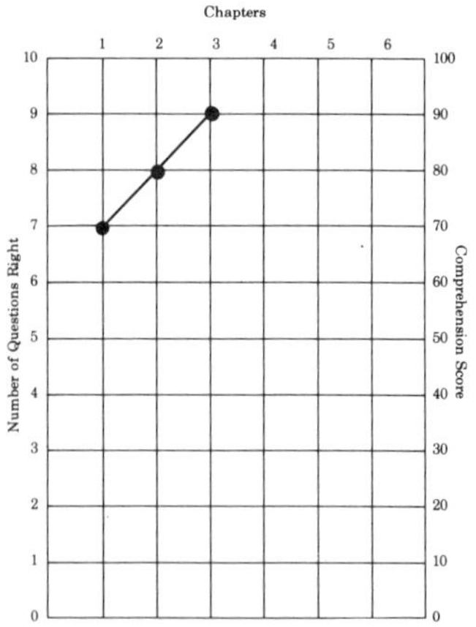

If the line between the dots on your graph does not go up, or if it goes down, see your instructor for help.

Comprehension Progress

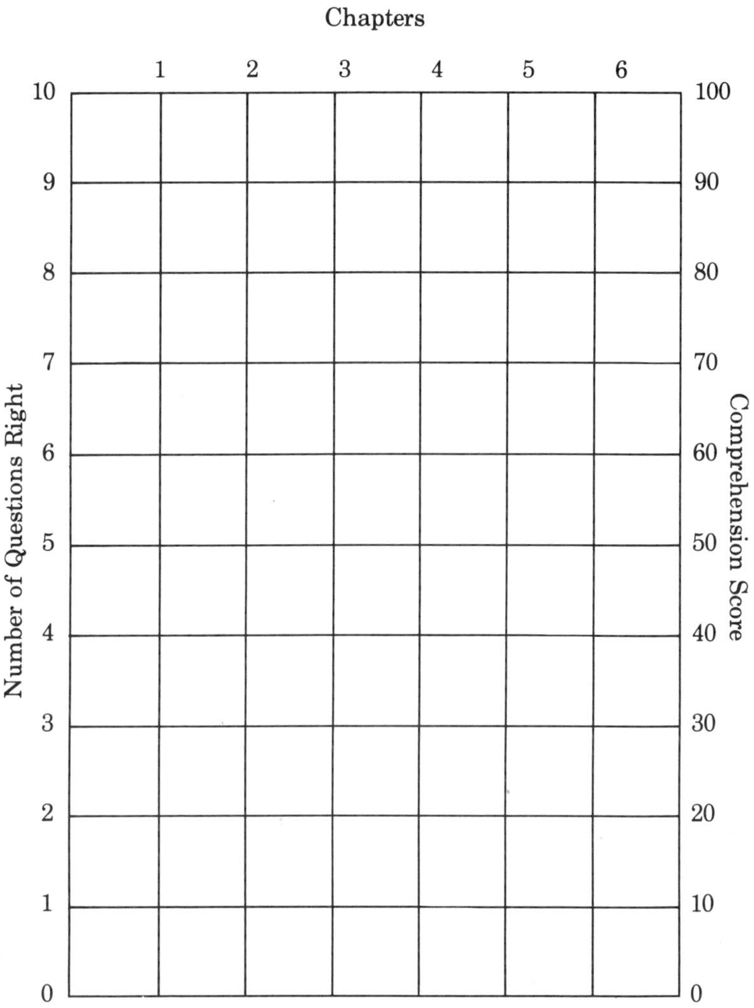

Skills Profile Graph

How to Use the Skills Profile Graph

1. There is a block on this graph for every comprehension question in the book.
2. Every time you get a question wrong, fill in a block which has the same letter as the question you got wrong. For example, if you get an A question wrong, fill in a block in the A row. Use the right row for each letter.

Look at the graph. It shows the profile of a student who got 3 questions wrong. This student got an A question wrong, a C question wrong, and a D question wrong.

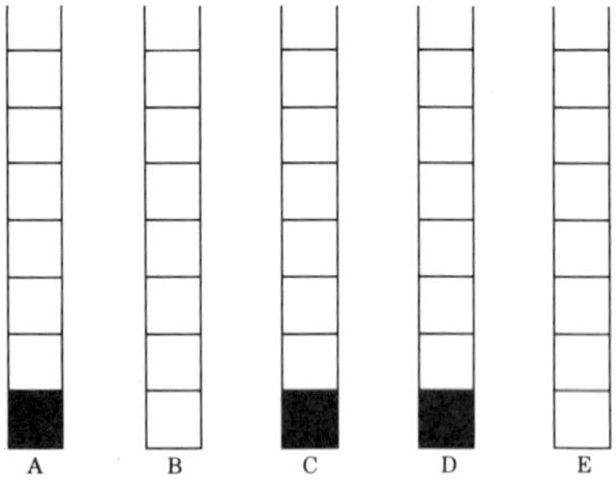

On the next chapter, this same student got 4 questions wrong and has filled in 4 more blocks.

The graph now looks like this. This student seems to be having trouble on question C. This shows a reading skill that needs to be worked on.

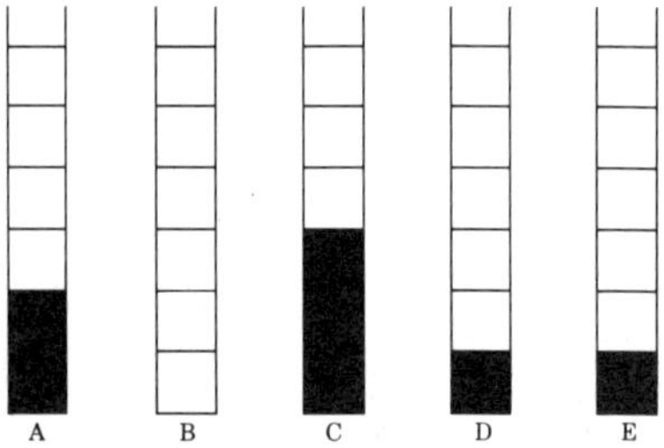

The blocks that are filled in on your graph tell you and your instructor the kinds of questions that give you trouble.

Look for the rows that have the most blocks filled in. These rows will be higher than the others. Talk to your instructor about them. Your instructor may want to give you extra help on these skills.

Skills Profile

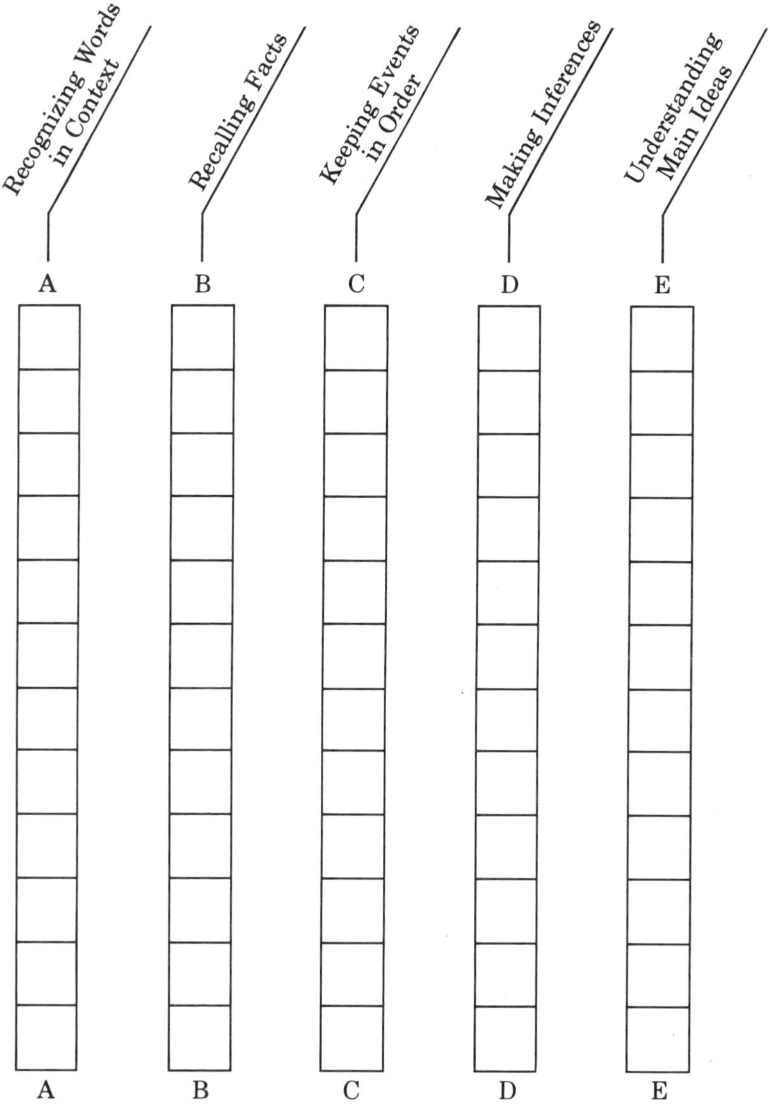